"You taste like frosting," Calder whispered

"Butter cream," _____ anted butter cream f_____

"Nice," he said, _____ u going to marry

"I can't—"

He didn't want to hear her refuse or argue, so he cut off her words with his mouth. His tongue swept across her lips and they parted for him. *Sweet,* he reflected, *and hot. Very hot.* It didn't take much for the two of them to ignite, a promising notion for the honeymoon. Warm, willing and passionate, Lisette dissolved in his arms. If only they were alone, he thought, wanting to feel her bare skin against his hands and mouth and—

"Mommy," a high-pitched voice interrupted. "Where do you want me to put the little groom figure?"

Calder whispered in Lisette's ear. "In the bride's bed, of course. What do you say?"

She laughed nervously. "No bride, no groom, no bed."

Calder groaned and released her, thinking of all the more interesting things he'd like to do than assemble a wedding cake.

"Watch the girls for me, please," she asked, searching his face.

Calder sighed. He was in over his head—in more ways than one. "No problem," he said, sounding braver than he felt. "It'll be a piece of cake."

Dear Reader,

Finding inspiration is sometimes painful and, occasionally, messy. I often clean when I am thinking about writing, but in the middle of the project I discover the answer to my creative dilemma and race back to the computer, which leaves behind half-finished cleaning chaos.

While thinking about the perfect woman for Calder Brown, I decided to clean my office bookshelves. Should I keep that collection of historical Christmas anthologies? Will I ever order *anything* from Victoria's Secret catalog? And wouldn't it be a good idea to rearrange my collection of Mary Balogh novels in their order of publication?

And then a small book fell on my head, bounced off the keyboard, hit the floor and sent the dogs running out of the room. Called *The French on Life and Love*, it contained a collection of French sayings, which became the immediate inspiration for the second book in my MONTANA MATCHMAKERS miniseries.

Voilà! I hope you enjoy Calder and Lisette's romance. For in the words of Nicolas Chamfort, "A day is wasted without laughter."

Kristine Rolofson

Books by Kristine Rolofson

MONTANA MATCHMAKERS
842—A Wife for Owen Chase (Aug. 2001)
850—A Bride for Calder Brown (Oct. 2001)
858—A Man for Maggie Moore (Dec. 2001)

KRISTINE ROLOFSON
A Bride for Calder Brown

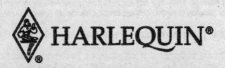

HARLEQUIN®

TORONTO • NEW YORK • LONDON
AMSTERDAM • PARIS • SYDNEY • HAMBURG
STOCKHOLM • ATHENS • TOKYO • MILAN • MADRID
PRAGUE • WARSAW • BUDAPEST • AUCKLAND

ISBN 0-373-25950-6

A BRIDE FOR CALDER BROWN

Copyright © 2001 by Kristine Rolofson.

All rights reserved. Except for use in any review, the reproduction or
utilization of this work in whole or in part in any form by any electronic,
mechanical or other means, now known or hereafter invented, including
xerography, photocopying and recording, or in any information storage
or retrieval system, is forbidden without the written permission of the
publisher, Harlequin Enterprises Limited, 225 Duncan Mill Road,
Don Mills, Ontario, Canada M3B 3K9.

All characters in this book have no existence outside the imagination of
the author and have no relation whatsoever to anyone bearing the same
name or names. They are not even distantly inspired by any individual
known or unknown to the author, and all incidents are pure invention.

This edition published by arrangement with Harlequin Books S.A.

® and TM are trademarks of the publisher. Trademarks indicated with
® are registered in the United States Patent and Trademark Office, the
Canadian Trade Marks Office and in other countries.

Visit us at www.eHarlequin.com

Printed in U.S.A.

1

"It's good manners to join in what everybody else is doing."
—*Stendhal (1783-1842)*

"I LOVE WEDDINGS. Success is such a wonderful thing and I'm glad we played our parts so well," Louisa declared, reaching for her tea cup with one hand while holding her cards in the other. Ella watched her twin dribble tea on the neatly pressed linen tablecloth and wondered if Lou would ever learn to hold her cup properly. At age eighty-one, one would think she'd know better.

"Lou," she said, frowning only a little. "You're spilling."

"Oh, dear," Louisa said, as she finally noticed the stains spreading across the white fabric. "There I go again."

"Careful. I can see your cards," Grace Whitlow, the third member of the Hearts Club, cautioned. And Missy Perkins, the youngest at seventy-six, patted the cloth with her own napkin.

"I'm sure if you soak it in cold water you'll have no trouble," she said.

"We have more tablecloths than that Martha Stewart," Louisa grumbled. "A few stains and spots aren't going to be any trouble. I can cut this up and use it for rags."

"You can never have enough rags," Grace agreed. She owned a bed-and-breakfast nearby, so she should know.

"We mustn't rest on our laurels," Ella said, steering the conversation back to the proper topic. "Just because we married off Owen Chase this morning doesn't mean we sit out the rest of the festival."

"What *are* laurels?" Missy tossed the deuce of clubs into the center of the table, signaling the beginning of the first round of Hearts, but no one answered her question. "And I thought we were here to celebrate our victory. They looked so happy, didn't they? And when Suzanne held that baby for the pictures..." she sighed. "It was such a *moment*. You are a marvel, Ella."

"Thank you." Ella, prepared for almost anything, carried a camera in her purse, which was something she wielded like a loaded gun. The thing came in handy, all right. She set a six of clubs onto the table. "I must admit, this has been one of my more successful days."

"I wonder if Cameron is going to be all right," Louisa murmured. She looked out the window toward their neighbor who had backed into a school bus that morning.

"The old fool is fine," Ella assured her. "Someone should take his driver's license away before he gets hurt or causes any more trouble."

"The bus slid on the icy road." Louisa looked at the others as she defended her friend. "There was black ice on Cam's driveway, too. It was an accident. It could have happened to anyone."

"Except it happened to someone who should be sitting in his La-Z-Boy recliner instead of behind the wheel of that old car." And to think, Louisa considered him one of the candidates for her own romance. Ella didn't know whether to laugh or cry at the thought of it. "Could we talk about finding a wife for Calder Brown now?"

The three women gasped, a collective inhalation of air that should have sucked all the oxygen out of the ornate Bliss dining room, a room whose décor had not changed since 1921. Missy recovered first.

"Calder? Are you serious? The man isn't even in town."

"He will be," Ella said. "He's going to find out that one of his best friends has been married and then he will return."

"Why?"

Louisa giggled. "Because everyone knows that Calder Brown throws the best bachelor parties."

"Not during the festival," Grace said. "He's never here during festival weeks."

"Owen is one of his best friends," Ella said. "Gabe will tell Calder and Calder will come home."

"I'd rather find a wife for Gabe," Missy said in a quiet voice. "It would be so much easier finding someone for a widower."

"In time," Ella told her. "But we need to make a list of available women for Calder Brown first. Any ideas?"

All three shook their heads.

"He's slept with most everyone in town," Grace offered. "Does that make it easier or harder to come up with a list of potential brides?"

"Easier," Ella said.

"Harder," Louisa said.

"Impossible," was Missy's response. "He's been with just about every available and interested woman under thirty-five and hasn't settled on one of them yet. We need new blood."

"Fresh meat."

Ella closed her eyes and prayed for patience before looking at her sister. "Wherever do you hear these phrases?"

"Well—"

"Never mind," she said, raising one hand as if to ward off the answer. "We need to come up with women for Calder. Any ideas?"

Once again they disappointed Ella with their silence.

"I guess I have to do everything around here," she sniffed, though the truth was she didn't know who to find for that wild young man either. "Get the phone book."

"You're going to call someone?"

"We're going to go through all of the names and see if anyone the least bit appropriate comes to mind."

"That's going to take all afternoon."

"I'll make a pitcher of margaritas," Louisa offered. "Just the thought of marrying off Calder makes me think we need alcohol."

Ella pretended to be annoyed, but the truth was she could use a drink herself.

GABE WAS THE ONE who told him. Calder sat on the king-size bed in one of the best rooms in Caesar's Palace and wished he hadn't returned his friend's phone call. Downstairs were blackjack tables, slot machines and more beautiful women than a man could believe existed in this world. If he hadn't come upstairs to change his shirt—one of the pretty cocktail waitresses had dropped a tray of drinks on him—he wouldn't have seen the message light blinking on the phone. He'd called Gabe back, of course, and now one of his best and oldest friends delivered the bad news.

"Owen got married," his best friend announced. "Met her last week in Ella Bliss's living room and married her this morning. Which means they'll be after *you* now. You'll get the invitation to tea, just like Owen did. So be prepared."

Calder Brown, the wealthiest bachelor in Bliss, shivered. There wasn't much he was afraid of, but the annual matchmaking festival rivaled the two things that could make his stomach knot up tighter than a bull's behind at fly time: rattlesnakes and overseas flights. And the thought of sitting in the Bliss ladies' house, fending off their good intentions, just about made him want to get on the next plane out of Vegas and head anywhere but home. And the farther away he went the better.

"Cal?"

"Yeah." If Gabe knew how afraid he was of Ella Bliss and her witchy friends, he'd never let him hear the end of it. Gabe O'Connor would laugh 'til he fell off his expensive horse, the one he'd won the last time he and Cal played poker. "I'm here."

"That's the problem. You're in Vegas and your friends are here. Expecting a party."

"It's a little late for a bachelor party. The man's on his honeymoon, I expect."

"Not yet. I think they're heading East at Christmas to meet her family next month, but for now they're settling in at Owen's place."

"Who's the bride?" He was stalling for time and they both knew it.

"No one you know, but she'll be good for him. She was a reporter from some magazine in New York and—"

"And the matchmakers struck again."

"Yeah." Gabe sounded as if he was laughing, damn him. "And you're next."

"No way. I'm on vacation."

"You've been gone for a month."

"Six weeks and two days."

"Whatever. You're not going to miss Chase's party."

"Because I'm the host?"

"Because you give the best parties," Gabe reminded him. "You always have. And this one's for Owen."

"I can't believe he got married," Cal grumbled. "I hope she's beautiful."

"She is," his friend assured him. "And Owen has

two kids to care for, so he can use all the help he can get."

"You've got two kids, but I don't see you rushing to the altar."

"Been there, done that," Gabe said, which was his standard reply. And Cal knew better than to push.

"What time is it?"

"Ten. In the morning."

"I'll catch a flight home today. Call Mac, will you, and warn him."

"What about Owen?"

"Tell him to keep Friday night open. He should be able to tear himself away from his bride for a few hours."

"No problem. I'll spread the word."

"Yeah," Calder said, before he hung up the phone. "You do that." He poured himself a whiskey and took a sip, then changed his mind. He'd have room service bring a large pot of coffee along with something for breakfast. He would need his wits about him as soon as he arrived home, because his father had taught him that the old ladies in town were dangerous as hell.

"HE SAID they're going to need the Big Cake," Mona said, hanging up the telephone. "I should have warned you there'd be lots of these parties going on."

Lisette Lemieux Hart, a young woman who prided herself on efficiency, took the pink slip of paper from her assistant's flour-covered fingers and frowned at the message scrawled there. "What kind of party?"

"A bachelor party, he said."

"Who said?"

"The man who called."

Lisette held the paper closer and studied the writing. "Mr. Boon?"

"Brown."

"Ah."

"Calder Brown's grandfather." Mona grinned, making her look younger than twenty. The niece of the former owner of the bakery, she had agreed to stay on when Lisette bought the place. The Dudleys had retired to a nearby town to be closer to their married daughter and their doctor, but Mona stayed in Bliss to keep her job and her boyfriend. And Lisette was glad for the help.

"I don't know who that is."

"Calder Brown of Three Forks Ranch? He's too old for me, but he's one of the best-looking men in town."

"The grandfather?" *Catered cold supper, chili, for*

twenty hungry men, she read. *Don't forget the Big Cake.*

"The grandson." Mona sighed. "He'll break your heart, so don't let him flirt with you too much."

Lisette wasn't interested in flirting. Or ranchers. Or handsome men, no matter what their ages. But she was interested in an assignment to cater a large party and provide a cake. "Why wouldn't he have Marryin' Sam cater the party? I'm not exactly known for my chili."

"They don't get along. Sam thought Cal was after his wife once."

"And was he?"

"Cal likes women, but he doesn't mess with the married ones. That's a good way to get shot at." Mona helped herself to a fat sugar cookie from the basket of cookies that had been too brown to sell. "A man can't be too careful."

"I see," Lisette said, but she wondered if she had made a mistake by moving her daughters to such a wild place. The realtor in Bozeman had assured her that Bliss was a family kind of town and the Dudley Bakery a good investment for a Frenchwoman who knew how to cook. Lisette had been more than happy to believe the saleswoman, especially since Bliss seemed light years away from Los Angeles. A woman and her children could disappear quite nicely here in Montana. And so they had. "What's the 'Big Cake'? Is there a special recipe somewhere?"

"The whole thing's downstairs in the basement somewhere. Uncle Joe used it a lot during festival season."

"Can you get it for me?" The matchmaking festival had been wonderful for business so far. She'd been deluged by women wanting gourmet coffee to drink while they sat in the windows and watched the men stroll past on the boardwalks. They'd bought chocolate petits fours and almond cookies and even the expensive pear tarts that were Lisette's specialty. They liked the Parisian style wrought iron tables and chairs, admired the sponged pastel walls and often asked Lisette how she remained so thin when she baked such wonderful pastries all day long.

Lisette could have told them, but she knew no one would believe her. Especially not during the festival. Women had their minds on love and their hearts set on romance. And if they wanted to spend thirty or forty minutes drinking cappuccino and sampling pastry, then so be it. Lisette told them she was from Paris and assured them all that it was the most romantic city in the world.

Next to Bliss, of course, they would say. And

everyone would laugh before the ladies ventured once again into the cold and wind of Montana in November.

Mona looked doubtful. "You'll have to come with me. It's pretty big."

"All right." She looked at her watch. Almost three o'clock and time to close up for the day. She'd been working since four-thirty this morning, but living in the apartment upstairs over the bakery solved a lot of problems. The girls loved the teenager who came at two o'clock and kept them occupied while their mother readied the bakery for the next day's work. And Mona—sweet, overweight and friendly—was a fountain of town and bakery information.

She locked the front door, turn the Closed sign to the outside and turned off the string of tiny white lights that threaded through the silk ivy strands that framed the large street-front windows.

Ten minutes later, Lisette learned what "Big Cake" really meant.

"MISS ELLA, I'M NOT—"

"Sit down, Calder," the elderly lady ordered, so Cal lowered himself carefully onto a couch that looked as if it belonged in a brothel. Miss Ella and Miss Louisa had never quite left the Victorian age,

Cal figured, which was another good reason to get the hell out of here as soon as possible.

"Ma'am?" He twirled the rim of his Stetson hat between his fingers and leaned forward, hoping the damn couch wouldn't collapse underneath him. Wouldn't be the first time. "I heard you wanted to see me before I headed home."

"You've been away," Ella declared, sitting in a chair across from him. She didn't look as though she approved. She had one of those long, gaunt faces that always looked like she was frowning. Her sister, on the other hand, was as plump as a summer rabbit and twice as fidgety. Louisa set a cup of tea on a tiny table near Cal's left elbow.

"I put a little whiskey in it," she whispered. "You look as if you could use it."

"Yes, ma'am." Calder picked up the cup and managed to swallow half of the hot drink before Ella demanded his attention again.

"You heard about Owen Chase," she said.

"Yes." He tried not to shudder. He even tried to look at Miss Ella and smile as if that was the best news he'd heard all month. "I hear he's a happy man."

"Yes, he is. Very happy. He met her here. *Here*," she repeated, giving him that beady-eyed stare.

"Right in this living room. Right there on that couch."

"Well, how about that." He drained the tea cup and hoped Miss Louisa would offer a second helping, but the younger Miss Bliss had settled herself beside him on the couch, whiskey and tea nowhere in sight.

"We had our doubts about the match," Miss Louisa admitted. "It was a week fraught with anxiety, but in the end true love prevailed. They were married on Tuesday. Sister and I were witnesses."

"That must have been quite a sight." Owen must have lost his mind—or been bamboozled by the Bliss ladies at last. And here Cal had always thought Owen such a sensible man.

"Quite gratifying, yes," Miss Ella agreed. She opened her mouth to speak again, but Cal was ready for her.

"Thanks for the tea," he said, setting the cup back in its flowered saucer. He made a move to rise, but Miss Louisa put her hand on his arm.

"Calder, dear, it's your turn."

"My turn?" He could feign ignorance and hope they would think he was too stupid for any woman to want to marry.

"You're at the top of the list," Ella announced. "So we need to know what kind of woman appeals to you." He must have looked stupid enough, because Ella frowned. "We need to know your *requirements*." Still stupid, he waited, fearing the worst. "For a *wife*, Calder."

"Miss Ella," Cal began, gripping his hat brim. "I don't want—"

"Doesn't matter what you want," the old witch answered, looking pleased with herself. "Love has a way of sneaking up on a man. Just ask your friend Owen. He's not at all displeased with the way things turned out. Have you met Suzanne?"

"Uh, no. I've got a present in the truck for them, but I haven't—"

"You're in for a grand surprise," Louisa said, beaming at him. "He wanted a redhead, so we got him one. It all worked out so well. She loved the baby, you know. Sat right here on this couch and held that baby and well," she said with a sigh, "Owen's fate was sealed."

"I'd like to leave my fate open," Cal said. He managed to get to his feet, but Ella Bliss rose to face him.

"A list, Calder. Your grandfather said you'd cooperate this year. He wants a great-grandson before he dies."

"Dies? He's never been sick a day in his life." Cal edged to the left, hoping he could get past the woman without accidentally knocking her over. All of a sudden he couldn't breathe very well. His shirt collar was damn near choking him.

"Just something to work with, dear," Miss Louisa said, following him. "Do you prefer blondes or brunettes?"

"Either."

"Tall, short or in between?"

"Doesn't really matter." What mattered was to get out of here as fast as he could. "I appreciate the help, ladies, but I'm not looking to get married right now."

"Of course you're not." Louisa patted his arm and made him feel guilty about being rude. Surely he could humor these old ladies for a few minutes. He looked down and smiled at her as if she was twenty-one and a *Baywatch* babe.

"Miss Louisa, I love women too much to settle down with just one."

"Ohh," she sighed. "My goodness."

"Oh, for heaven's sake," the skinny sister sputtered. "You're not getting any younger, Calder Brown. It's time to grow up."

"Grow up?" Cal turned to stare at her. "Why in he—ck would I want to do that?"

2

"After all, the world is but an amusing theater, and I see no reason why a pretty woman should not play a principal part in it."
—Countess du Barry (1746-1793)

"MRS. HART? We have a wee bit of a problem," Mr. Brown declared, rubbing his beefy hands together nervously. Lisette wanted to take the dear old man by the hand and assure him that everything would be fine. The ranch house kitchen was magnificent, with modern oversize appliances and plenty of counter space, as if it had been designed by a chef. In fact, it was so far away from the living area that the huge room had most likely been added on to the original massive log house.

"We've plenty of food, I hope?" She'd assembled tray after tray of cold cuts, knowing that men preferred to make their own sandwiches. And the recipe she'd used for chili had won prizes at the Texas State Fair, or so the cookbook said. She'd displayed bottles of hot sauce, just in case there were those men who enjoyed burning their throats while eating.

"The food's not the problem, ma'am." He filled two glasses of champagne and set one on the counter for her. "Please. Join me."

"Thank you. Then what is it? I'm sure we can figure something out." Lisette fiddled with a tray of pickles, olives and hot peppers until she was satisfied they looked appetizing, then looked up at the elderly gentleman who had been so helpful these past four hours. The younger Mr. Brown, the one who charmed all the ladies, had been nowhere to be seen, though she thought she saw him unloading kegs of beer from the back end of a pickup truck a couple of hours ago. From the back he'd looked harmless enough, yet strong and virile and very accustomed to carrying kegs of beer from one place to another.

"It's the cake, ma'am."

Lisette wanted to laugh, but Mr. Brown looked terribly serious. The Big Cake had turned out to be exactly that, a huge three-tiered "cake" made of plywood and mounted on a wheeled platform. The top of the cake was hinged, allowing someone—a woman, of course—to pop out and entertain the party goers. Right now it sat in a corner of the huge room awaiting its turn in the spotlight. "What's wrong with the cake?"

"It's not the cake. It's the entertainment." He sat down in one of the oversize chairs parked around a large table. "She's not coming."

"Who isn't—oh, no," Lisette said, as she realized who "she" was. The cake-ee. "What happened?"

"Terrie—she's one of the bartenders at the Wedding Bell Blues—was supposed to do it, but she eloped with the basketball coach this afternoon. She called from Nevada to say she was sorry, but in the excitement of getting married she forgot all about Calder's party."

"No problem, Mr. Brown. I brought a real cake," Lisette said. She remembered the glass of champagne he'd poured for her and reached for the glass. She took a sip and wasn't disappointed.

"But we need a real woman."

That's when she caught on to the real problem. "I'm a caterer. A baker. I don't jump out of cakes."

"You're small enough to fit in there just fine, ma'am."

"I don't—" She wanted to say she didn't do whatever it was women who jumped out of cakes did at bachelor parties, but she didn't want to embarrass the old man. "I can't dance," she managed to stammer. "Or anything else."

Mr. Brown shook his head. "You don't have to dance, honey. You just have to pop out of the cake and wish Owen a happy birth—no, that's not it. Hell, I can't remember what song Calder plays at the bachelor parties. You don't have to do anything but kiss the groom and wave to the boys and then serve the *real* cake."

"Mr. Brown—"

"I know it's not your job, Mrs. Hart, but I'd sure appreciate your assistance."

"I really can't—"

"And," he continued, as if he hadn't heard her refusal, "it's *tradition*."

"Tradition," she repeated, looking back at the cake while she sipped her champagne. Battered and gauche, the wooden cake sat ready for an occupant. A sexy female occupant. Once again Lisette struggled not to laugh. "That old cake has seen a lot of parties, hasn't it."

"Yes, ma'am," he said, finishing his glass and reaching across the table for another bottle. "We've got a fine matchmaking tradition in this town, all right. Have you seen the dress?"

"No." There'd been a box stored inside the cake, but Lisette hadn't examined the black lace contents too closely. Now she went over to the cake and retrieved the box.

"Well, bring it over here. You're a little thing, so you won't have any trouble fittin' into it."

"Mr. Brown," she tried again, but the old man was too fast for her.

"Call me Mac," he said, giving her a wink. "You pop out of that cake, honey, and I'll personally see to it that that bakery of yours has all the business it can handle. And I'll bet those two daughters you were talking about would like their own ponies."

"They've never ridden horses, Mac."

"They could."

"Thank you, but—"

"Mrs. Hart, are you trying to make an old man beg? Cal won't be happy with his old grandpa if I mess up his party. He thinks a lot of Owen and there's no finer man in the whole county than Owen Chase, raisin' those orphaned nieces of his. Least we could do is figure out how to pop out of a cake and wish him well." With that long speech over, Mac drained another glass of champagne.

"Orphaned nieces?" Lisette walked over and sat down across from Mac, setting the unopened box on the table next to the champagne.

"Very sweet, they are, too," he said, topping off her glass. "One's only a babe."

"He must be a very special man," Lisette said, taking another drink of the expensive champagne.

She'd always liked champagne, especially with a strawberry nestled in the bottom of the glass. Too bad there were no fresh strawberries in Montana this time of year. "When is he getting married?"

"Oh, Owen already did, on Tuesday. Married a reporter who came here from New York to do a story on the festival. I heard she likes children."

"Good for him. And for her." She really should fix another tray of appetizers, just in case the men ran out. She could hear distant laughter, country western music and the low hum of conversation, but she had yet to meet the infamous host. A couple of young ranch hands had been carrying the trays back and forth, due to the "no females" edict from the boss. "Mr. Brown—"

"Mac," he reminded her.

"Mac." Lisette tried to resist his pleading look. She wished she could make him understand her reluctance without hurting his feelings. "I'm a *mother*."

"Then look at it this way, how many chances will you have to pop out of a cake?"

It was a reasonable question. She sipped her champagne and considered it. After all, how much dignity did she have left in her life? Not much, considering she'd been falsely married to a man who had two other wives and had been caught while angling for two more. The tabloids had loved the story and before she'd changed her phone number, the calls from the talk shows had been constant. She'd been a fool, blissfully content to believe anything her so-called husband had told her to explain his many absences. When the truth came out, she'd protected herself and her children and found a town far, far away from that humiliating part of her life.

Which had nothing to do with whether or not she should climb out of a cake.

"I can't," she said, but she sounded weak even to her own ears and the old man knew it. He grinned at her and poured them each another glass of champagne.

"Sure you can, honey. You'll knock 'em dead."

Lisette reached over and opened the box. The costume was black, all right, except for the little red satin rosettes around the neckline. She lifted it from the tissue paper and began to laugh.

If Calder Brown considered this sexy, there was something wrong with the man.

"You've got a deal, Mac," Lisette said. "But just this once, because it's an emergency."

"Deal," the man said, grinning. He took her hand but, instead of shaking it, he planted a kiss on the back of her hand. "You'll do just fine."

Lisette had her doubts about that, but never let it be said that she didn't keep her end of a bargain.

"I HEAR YOU'RE NEXT," Owen said, taking the beer Cal handed him.

"Next?"

"To get married. The Bliss sisters are after you now," Owen explained.

"Lord help me," Cal muttered. "I did the 'tea in the living room' thing with them the day before yesterday, but they didn't get anywhere. I made it clear I'm not looking for a bride." Somehow he didn't think that Ella or Louisa had believed him—or had changed their minds about matchmaking for him.

"It's not the worst thing that can happen, you know."

He took another swallow of beer before answering. "Spoken like a happily married man."

His friend beamed. "Yeah."

"Word is you've married a special lady," Cal said, wondering at Owen's pleased expression. Yet the man had always been fairly calm and quiet, the reserved one of the three close friends, and the shy one with the ladies. Gabe was the stubborn one, a keg of dynamite under the contained exterior. Right now he was playing bartender in the corner of the living room with the built-in liquor cabinet, counter and sink. A stranger would never know to look at him that he was a family man, raising kids and running a business and keeping the women at arm's length.

"You'll have to meet her," Owen said. "Soon."

"I'll come over one day next week. I've been driving around with the wedding gift in the truck."

"Come by any time," Owen said. "And see what married life is like."

Cal shook his head. "It's all yours, pal. I haven't met a woman yet I could see living with forever."

"It'll happen," Owen promised. "When you least expect it." Calder didn't know what was the matter with him...or anyone else, for that matter.

Gabe waved to get Cal's attention, then gave him the thumbs-up sign.

"Get ready," Cal told Owen. "We're about to check out the entertainment."

"Not the cake," Owen groaned. "Who'd you talk into getting inside of the damn thing this time?"

"Wait and see."

Mac wheeled the cake into the living room, while the guests sang "For He's a Jolly Good Fellow," a song everyone knew the words to.

"Open it," he told Owen, but his friend shook his head.

"I'm a married man," he said, as Mac stopped the

cake in front of him. "I only came to play poker for a while and let you guys give me a hard time."

"We played poker," Gabe said. "Now we're singing."

"Can't have a bachelor party without a cake," someone called, and several others hollered their agreement.

"I'll do the honors," Cal said, and he reached over and lifted the hinged lid. And then his heart threatened to stop beating and Cal had to remind himself to breathe.

He told himself it was the surprise, that's all. He'd expected Terrie, a good-natured bartender with a wild streak and a bawdy sense of humor, but the woman who appeared from the top of the cake was no one he'd ever seen before. This woman wore the black outfit like a princess. A very lithe, sexy princess. Her long dark hair tumbled past her shoulders and hid most of her small breasts. He cursed the dated outfit for its modesty; maybe during World War II it had been considered risqué, but not at present. Yet…what the outfit didn't show was what intrigued him.

"Are you the groom?" she asked, her voice tinged with an accent he couldn't identify.

"No," Calder said, and her lips tilted in amusement. Her eyes were an unusual shade of emerald green, almost as black as the eyelashes that fringed them.

"Then who are you?"

For the life of him, he couldn't remember his name. And then it came to him, through the enthusiastic cheers of his guests.

"Cal," he replied.

"Cal whom?"

"My name. Cal. Short for Calder." Any expertise he thought he had with women vanished as if he were twelve years old again and blackmailed into skinny-dipping in Maggie Dexter's pond.

She gave him her hand and he helped her climb out of the cake while Garth Brooks sang "I've Got Friends in Low Places" and the men whistled their approval at the lady's outfit. The black lace-covered top was sleeveless, the kind of fabric that stretched and clung to a woman's curves. He'd seen other women in the same outfit maybe fifty times or more. But this woman wore it differently. The skirt was some kind of fancy mesh, so he could see a pair of shapely legs encased in black tights underneath the skirt. When the woman brushed her hair away from her face, she revealed an enticing swell of breasts above little red roses.

And the other men noticed, though none were rude about enjoying the view, Cal wished they'd all go blind. He lifted his gaze from those lovely, perfect breasts and guided her toward Owen. "The groom."

"Congratulations," she said, and leaned forward to kiss the man's cheek. "I hear you're a very fortunate man."

"Yes, ma'am," Owen said, smiling at her. "Thanks for coming to the party."

"You're welcome." She took him by the hand and led him through the crowd to where Mac stood beside a large cake, a real one this time. The top tier held a cowboy groom and his bride. Both china figures wore boots. "I brought you a real cake. You're to take this section home to your wife."

"She'll like that," Owen said.

Cal positioned himself very close to her. As close as he dared. He told himself he wanted her only because she was a stranger.

He told himself he couldn't have her.

And told himself of course he could. All he had to do was try. And try again. Until she was in his bed and happy to be there, too, as every other woman had been. Of course, he only picked the willing women, so the odds were in his favor right from the start.

She turned to look up at him. "Do you want

me—" She paused, as if trying to interpret his expression. "To cut the cake now, Mr. Brown?"

"I want you," was what he heard himself say. Lucky for him she didn't hear him. Someone had turned the music up and the men began to sing along with another of Garth's songs. "Yeah," he said, nodding. "Go ahead."

He watched her walk behind the table as if she was presiding over a Chamber of Commerce meeting. Mac, preening as if assisting a duchess, gave her a choice of knives and, when she selected the appropriate one, she set out to cut the cake in neat slices, as if she'd done so a thousand times. She couldn't be a stripper, not with that tiny body. And she wasn't from Bliss or he would have met her before now. A friend of Terrie's, perhaps, in town for the festival? A dancer from Bozeman?

He moved toward his grandfather, who would know the details. "Tell me she's not a stripper," he said, keeping his voice low. "And where in hell is Terrie?"

Mac moved away from the table, leaving the woman to serve slices of cake to a group of men who would rather have chips and beer. But Cal heard them talking to her about cinnamon rolls and apple tarts as if they were all gourmet chefs. "Terrie eloped last night. And no, this one's not a stripper."

"Then who is she?"

"A decent woman," his grandfather snapped. "And she's not going to dance or take off her clothes or tell jokes. She's going to serve cake."

"Like the queen of England."

"Yep."

"Good." He ignored the look of disapproval Mac gave him and watched the dark-haired woman serve cake to men who were behaving like little boys trying not to misbehave at a tea party.

"Leave her alone," his grandfather growled. "She's divorced, raising kids on her own, working hard to make ends meet. I figure she's got enough problems."

Cal smiled to hide his unusual attack of nerves. "Then I'll make her forget them."

SHE DIDN'T KNOW what she'd been so nervous about. All in all, climbing out of a cake was an appropriate—if a little dramatic—entrance for a baker. The costume was less revealing than a bathing suit and about as sexy as the average cocktail dress. She might keep the "Big Cake" in the front of her shop, fill it with flowers or twine little white lights around it and advertise wedding cakes.

A town like this obviously needed wedding cakes and she'd had little chance to advertise that particular creation to the townspeople of Bliss. No one needed to know that this was the very first wedding cake she'd made since culinary class.

"You're very welcome," she told the last man in line after the tall cowboy thanked her for the slice of white cake with lemon filling and fluffy vanilla frosting.

And then the very handsome man named Cal came back, the one who owned the house and was paying for the party. He smiled down at her with those dark eyes of his and that sensual smile he knew very well affected any woman with an ounce of estrogen in her bloodstream. She was supposed to feel attracted to him, and she did.

Though she knew better.

But there was something about stepping out of a cake, acting as a cowboy sex symbol for an hour instead of an overworked, overtired baker and divorced—if she could be divorced from someone she was never legally married to—mother of two.

"I don't know your name," the man said.

"Would you like a piece of cake?" Lisette picked up a dessert plate piled high with cake and deliberately ignored the man's curiosity.

"Your accent," he said. "Italian?"

"French." She held the plate towards him. "Go ahead, *monsieur*. Enjoy."

He took the plate from her hand, surprising her with his careful avoidance of her fingers. "And now you live—where?"

"Mrs. Hart?" The elderly Mr. Brown came up beside her. "Is my grandson flirting with you?"

"Of course," Lisette answered, looking back at Cal. "And he is about to try my dessert."

His eyebrows rose. "*Your* dessert?"

"Yes."

"You made this?"

"Yes. I catered your party."

"You live here, in Bliss?"

Once again she replied, "Yes. With my daughters." Then she turned away from him and began to gather up the dirty dishes. He rattled her more than she wanted to admit. Had it been that long since a man looked at her as if she was a pear tart and he hadn't eaten in months? She tried to remember when a man had last touched her, but nothing came to mind. She didn't need the complications of a man in her life, was operating perfectly well without a husband, and certainly didn't want the emotional complications of taking a lover.

But, oh, to be made love to would be nice. Just for a little while to feel alive and passionate, to touch someone else's bare, smooth skin and run her fingers along a wide chest covered with soft hair.

"Mrs. Hart?"

Lisette blinked. Calder Brown stood in front of her, his own very wide chest only inches away. "Yes?"

"Are you all right?"

"Never better, Mr. Brown." She took a step sideways in order to move around him and get to the kitchen. It was the outfit's fault, Lisette decided. The silly thing had made her feel unlike herself. It had reminded her that she was a woman.

Which was not exactly a good thing.

He followed her through the crowd of men and across the wide living room. He was behind her down the enormous hallway that led to the kitchen. And when she had finished stacking the plates on the counter beside the sink, she turned to see him standing there, his hands full of dishes and his expression full of longing.

"Go away," was all she could think of to say.

"I thought I'd help."

"You can't. It's not your job."

"It's my house," he pointed out, setting the plates down on the counter. "I can do what I want."

"And I'm sure you do," Lisette said.

"You're not wearing shoes."

"I didn't know I'd be hopping out of a cake tonight."

"Do you do it often?"

"This was my first time." She looked down at her costume. "And my last, too."

"It was that bad?"

"It wasn't what I expected." She opened the dishwasher and began to load the dirty plates. "I've never been to a bachelor party before."

"You're welcome to come back to the ranch anytime," the man told her. "I'll give you the ten dollar tour."

Mac hurried into the kitchen, a large tray full of dirty glasses in his hands. "You'd better get out there," he told his grandson. "Owen is getting ready to head home to his bride and the rest of them are getting ready to go to town and see what's going on."

"I was just telling Mrs. Hart to come back sometime and we'd show her the ranch."

Mac nodded. "I'm giving her girls riding lessons one of these days." He set the tray down on the island. "Mrs. Hart, don't bother cleaning up. The boys will give me a hand later."

"I hate to leave a mess."

"Leave?" Cal frowned.

She looked for a clock and found it on the wall above a long row of windows. She had another hour before the baby-sitter expected her to return. "I need to put away the food first," she said, moving a tray of appetizers toward the refrigerator. "And pack up my supplies."

"I'll help," the rancher said, surprising his grandfather, who snorted. "Just give me a few minutes. I'll be back."

"Why?" she asked, staring at his back as he left the kitchen. He really was the handsomest man she'd seen in a very long time.

Which was a shame. Lisette didn't have much use for handsome men. Or, if she thought about it, any kind of men except the ones who were too old to cause trouble.

3

"Passion never reasons."
—Countess du Barry

"DON'T SEDUCE THE HELP."

"I can't hear you." Cal smiled, hoping his grandfather would quit looking at him like he had just burned down the barn, but Mac didn't smile at Cal's attempt to ignore him.

"She's a respectable woman," he grumbled. "Not one of the gals at the bar. Don't mess with her unless you're serious."

"Serious? How can I be serious? An hour ago I helped her out of a *cake*."

"And now you're following her around like you're a hunting dog and she's the pheasant."

"It's the fishnet stockings," Cal explained, half-joking. "Mrs. Hart has a pair of beautiful legs. Exactly how much beer have you had tonight, Gramps?" He liked to call Mac that sometimes, especially when they were alone and the old man was fussing at him for something.

"Not enough," the old man sighed. "I like the lady. But she's too good for you."

"Thanks for the heartwarming compliment. It's nice to know I'm loved." He drained the last of the beer in his glass and tossed the empty cup into the trash. A couple of guys were finishing up the last round of poker, Owen and a big box of cake had been sent home to the new Mrs. Chase, and the rest of the guests had headed down to the Wedding Bell Blues for more beer and a look at the new women in town for the festival. Cal was supposed to head down there himself, having been assured that the dreaded Bliss sisters never ventured into the local bars to further their matchmaking plans.

"Son, you've been loved too damn much."

Which made for excellent memories in his old age, Cal figured. Not that he wasn't going to be out of his prime for a long, long time. The Browns were known for living way into old age—all except Cal's father, who had the damn bad luck to get kicked in the head by an ornery horse.

Mac wasn't done with his grumbling. "It's about time you settled down and started having sons of your own. We're gonna need a few to run this ranch one of these days."

"Yep," Cal agreed, having heard this lecture

more times than he could count. "I'm only thirty, so I figure I've got about fifteen years of freedom left."

"I'll be dead then. And not happy about it, either."

"Well, I don't blame you," Cal said. "Take the boys and get on down to the Blues so you can get a table before the tourists take 'em all." Mac's legs couldn't take standing at the bar for more than half an hour. "I'll help the lady load up her things and I'll meet you down there."

"Make sure you get a bill from her so I can pay her first thing in the morning," his grandfather said. "And mind your manners."

"I will," Cal promised before heading down the hall. He sure didn't mind having an excuse to see the pretty caterer once again. He'd returned to the kitchen once before and watched as she packed uneaten food in plastic bags, all the while exclaiming rapturously to Mac about his oversize refrigerator and going out of her way to ignore the man who owned the damn appliance. Surely she must be finished now.

He wondered if she wanted to go down to the Blues and have a drink with them. He would buy her a beer and show the lady a good time. It was the least he could do for a woman who could make a fifty-year-old outfit look sexy.

"Aw, SHOOT. You took it off."

Lisette turned from the sink to see the disappointment on the rancher's handsome face. Changing into her official chef's outfit had been a good idea. Lisette felt more prepared to finish cleaning the kitchen and load her equipment into the van when she didn't look like a floozy. She also felt better able to withstand Calder Brown's flirting comments.

"The party's over," she reminded him, waving one hand toward the pile of dirty dishes she was in the middle of rinsing. She pretended her heart wasn't beating faster and visions of that man's mouth on hers weren't teasing her brain. "The coach has turned back into a pumpkin and Cinderella has left the building."

"Who?"

"I guess you don't read fairy tales." She turned back to the dishes and set a stack of them in the sink filled with soapy water.

"I was raised on Zane Gray and A. B. Guthrie," he informed her. "Every once in a while I'd find one of Mac's *Playboy* magazines, but not often enough."

She wondered if he was teasing her. He looked like the type who would. "My daughters and I prefer fairy tales." She tried to ignore how close he stood and tried to change the subject to more professional topics. "How was the chili? Were you satisfied with it?"

"It was real interesting," he said. "I've never had chili without beans before. The beef was real tender, though. And the men seemed to like it."

"Good." The pot was empty, she wanted to point out. They "seemed to like it" so much Lisette had had to refill the tureen four times.

"I'd like to thank you for your hard work," the man drawled. "Thought we could go down to the Wedding Bell Blues and have a drink or two."

"No, thanks."

"It's not wild or anything like that," he assured her, at the same time stacking dishes as if he'd done it all his life. He must have noticed her surprise, because he said, "My mother taught me how to clean up a kitchen."

"Has your company left?"

"Sure have." He frowned. "You don't have to clean all of this," he said. "I've got a couple of men who can take care of it in the morning."

"I don't leave a messy kitchen. It's not professional."

"Oh."

She tried not to smile and kept her attention on loading the dishwasher until it was full. That left the pots—her pots, which she decided to take home dirty and clean later—and wiping off the stovetop and counters. If she hurried she could get out of here earlier than she'd planned. Maybe the girls would be asleep and she could have a long hot bubble bath and read the new issue of *Bon Appétit*.

It wasn't the rancher's fault that she turned around and crashed into him. It wasn't his fault that her body reacted instinctively, freezing her in place against him with the most intimate part of her anatomy pressed against his rock-hard thigh. His very *warm* thigh.

And it wasn't his fault that she couldn't speak for a second or two, not even when he reached out to grab her arm so she wouldn't fall over. The sponge flew out of her fingers and careened into his chest before dropping to the tiled floor. And Calder Brown, the handsome rancher, naturally took advantage of the situation by drawing the upper half of her body into his, so that she was pressed very nicely against all that male strength.

He dropped his head and kissed her. Lisette didn't close her eyes, but she saw that he closed his. She was too surprised to move, too shocked by the lovely, heated sensation centered between her legs. She'd thought that part of her would remain numb for life. His lips were cool and strangely gentle, as if testing her response. She thought she might have leaned against him, and maybe her free arm lifted so her fingers could curve around his shoulder. He had a very hard shoulder.

And a wonderful way of moving his lips against hers. Lisette remembered making love with her husband—the lying traitor—but she didn't remember ever having been kissed like this, with this kind of reaction bubbling through her body. There was nothing else to do but push him away before she ended up spread-eagled on the floor.

He smiled down at her, but he didn't let her go. "I've never kissed a cook before," he said.

"You might want to watch yourself. I'm very skilled with a paring knife." She hoped he wouldn't notice that she was having trouble catching her breath.

"Sweetheart, I don't frighten easily," the man warned, sounding amused at the thought of anyone thinking he could be afraid.

"Well, I thought I should mention it," Lisette murmured. "Just in case you wanted to have children some day." What was the matter with her? She was actually having *fun*, for heaven's sake. At least it felt fun, in an crazy way. Of course Lisette should have known better than to flirt. It was the outfit, of course. There had been something about the black lace that had fired up the man's libido. Or maybe kissing women in his kitchen was something he did often.

He was a very practiced kisser.

"I don't think you'll hurt me," the man drawled. "My feelings, maybe, but my, uh, private parts? Nah." He drew her closer, so Lisette felt the size and hardness of one particular private part against her abdomen.

Never in her life had she considered having a one-night stand, but here she stood on a Friday night in Montana actually wondering what it would be like to make love to Calder Brown.

Just for a little while, she mused. Just so she remembered what it was like to feel passion. To feel wanted.

To feel like a flaming idiot.

"I can't," she said, then flushed when she realized she'd spoken aloud.

"Can't what?" His large palm stroked her back, massaging muscles sore from bending over counters and lifting heavy pans. Lisette rested her forehead against his chest and gave in to the back rub.

"Can't let you do this." She pulled away and he dropped his arms and let her step back.

"Do what?"

"Rub my back."

"You were enjoying it. I think I heard you moan."

"I didn't moan."

"Maybe it was me." He grinned. "You have a beautiful back, but your muscles are tight."

"My muscles and I are going home."

He looked disappointed. "But we were just starting to get to know each other."

"I shouldn't have let your grandfather talk me into drinking champagne with him." She turned back to the sink and stuck her hands back in the water. She would scrub the last pot free of chili remnants and then she would drive as fast as she could toward town without being reckless.

"That's how he talked you into wearing that outfit?" Calder handed her the sponge that had fallen to the floor.

"That was part of it." She rinsed the pot under hot running water and then set it in the drainer on the counter.

"And the other part?" Cal picked up a dishtowel again and gave the pot a few swipes with it before setting it on the island counter behind him.

"I saw the outfit," she explained, letting the water out of the drain.

"You did it justice."

Lisette smiled. "It must have seemed pretty glamorous after World War II."

"Everyone begged the Dudleys to replace it," he

explained. "But if you wanted the Big Cake, you got that costume and nothing else, unless it was less revealing. One time my father popped out of it in his long red underwear. It was my mother's birthday and he did it in the middle of a ladies' luncheon in town."

"I see where you get your sense of humor." She took the dishtowel out of his hands and dried her own. Then she moved away, to finish packing up her supplies.

"Are you sure you won't have a drink with me?" He reached out and took her hand, stopping her from moving out of reach.

"I can't," she said, liking him despite the flirting. Or maybe because of it. No one had flirted with her since she was seventeen.

"Okay. Let me help you with that," he offered, dropping her fingers in order to take the cardboard box she'd filled with her equipment. "Will you at least tell me your name?"

"Lisette," she said over her shoulders as she retrieved her new down jacket from the back of a chair and grabbed two shopping bags of empty plastic containers. With Calder's help, she loaded the van in three trips, the final one carrying the wooden cake.

The trouble started back in the kitchen, when Lisette made one last check of the room to make sure she hadn't left anything behind or anything out of place. The house was quiet, the only noise coming from the hum of the dishwasher in its rinse cycle. It was crazy to be so aware of the man standing next to her.

"Wait," he said, his hand on the knob for the outside door. "Mac wanted to make sure you left him the bill."

"It's here," she said, realizing she'd forgotten the most important part of the evening. Just another reason to keep her mind off cowboys and her focus on business. "In my bag." She hoisted the heavy tote from her shoulder and went to set it on the table, but in her haste to cover her embarrassment, she missed the table. Well, not all of it, she realized. But enough that the tote tipped over and its contents spilled to the floor. Lisette caught the bag before it fell off the table to join the rest of the mess.

"Oh," was all she could say.

"Whoa," was all Calder spoke, as papers, pens, notebooks, lipstick, crayons, markers and a pink Polly Pocket locket scattered across the tile floor.

Lisette dropped to her knees to retrieve her things before she could embarrass herself any further. It was one thing to let herself kiss the man, but another to act clumsy and nervous when she was within minutes of making her getaway.

Life really wasn't fair, Lisette decided. Because instead of waiting impatiently at the door as some men would have—her idiot sort-of-husband a perfect example—Calder Brown dropped down to his haunches and began gathering up the papers that had scattered like dried leaves around the table leg.

"Secret recipes?"

"If I tell you I'll have to kill you," she quipped, hoping to sound casual and undisturbed by how close he was to her once again.

He studied the paper. "I can't read your writing."

"It's in French," she said.

"I'm impressed." She noticed that he was looking at her mouth and not her recipes.

"Don't get too excited. It's my grandmother's handwriting." She noticed that he shifted his weight so he was leaning closer to her. In fact, he looked as if he intended to kiss her again, the realization of which sent a little shiver of anticipation down Lisette's spine. She knelt back on her heels and tried to concentrate on the conversation. "I'm working on translating her recipes."

"Admirable," he said. "Keep the cooking secrets in the family."

"I'd like..."

He took the papers out of her hand, lifted the tote bag from her lap and proceeded to take her by the shoulders.

"You'd like?" he prompted.

"To write a cookbook," she managed to say before he kissed her thoroughly. She shouldn't have enjoyed it so much, shouldn't have leaned forward to meet him, and definitely shouldn't have curled her arms around his neck, because she tipped him over.

And she ended up laying on top of him, their legs tangled, her hand wedged between the back of his neck and the floor.

"I'm sorry," she said. "I overreacted."

"You're a very interesting woman," Cal replied, lifting his head so she could free her hand. He rearranged his legs so that she was lying on top of him without breaking any limbs—his or hers.

"I'm not really like this," she confessed. "This is a very odd night."

"It's about to get odder," Calder Brown agreed. "I think we're about to make out under my kitchen table." He paused and looked hopeful. "Unless you'd consider moving to my bedroom."

She shook her head. "Too dangerous."

"That's one word for it, I guess. Sweetheart, only

a few layers of clothing keeps us from making this pretty damn satisfying."

"I know." Lisette sighed and contemplated the intriguing cleft in his chin. Chins were safer than contemplating the evidence of Cal's arousal against her abdomen. Lord, she was growing warmer by the second. "I'm trying to talk myself out of doing anything immoral, foolish or embarrassing."

"I think you can cross off embarrassing," he said, easing his large hands under the chef's jacket, under the white tank top, to caress her bare back. "Kiss me while you think about the others."

She did kiss him, which was what led to the slow and steady removal of her clothing. She even helped, because by the time his hands roamed to her breasts she was a lost woman.

"Foolish," she murmured, to which he rolled her gently onto her back.

"Nope. I have a condom in my wallet," he answered, and with that her slacks were unzipped and slid down her legs, and Lisette kicked them off.

"Immoral?"

"Neither one of us is married," he replied, popping a button off his shirt as he pulled it off and tossed it aside. He had the most wonderful chest, with generous hair that made her want to rub her fingers into it and then maybe her nose. And mouth.

"No," she said, reaching for him. Not married. Never married. Not really.

"Engaged?" he asked.

"No. You?"

"Never even thought about it."

She didn't know how he managed to unzip his jeans, unbuckle his belt and shove jeans and jockey shorts down his thighs and off his body while he continued to kiss her. He rained kisses on her mouth, her bare shoulder, her left breast and lower, to the ticklish dip of her waist before settling his naked body on top of hers in the most satisfying way. He was hard muscle, rough skin, clean-smelling and intriguing male, right down to the impressive length of him nestled between her thighs. That part was pure pulsing heat. Lisette felt it and, to her guilty delight, wanted it inside of her.

"Now," was all she had to say.

His eyebrows rose, those eyes looking down into hers with surprise.

"I don't think I want to wait," she explained, trying not to wriggle against him so he wouldn't think she was some kind of sex maniac.

"I know the feeling," Calder murmured, but he dipped his head and tickled her right nipple with the tip of his tongue. "Wait one second longer," he said, reaching for his discarded jeans. He managed to get his wallet out of the pocket and find a small packet, then with an experienced ease Lisette found reassuring, he slid the condom on before settling his body on top of hers once again.

She lifted her arms to his shoulders as he eased himself inside of her slowly, as if giving her body time to adjust and stretch to accommodate him. Lisette couldn't help sighing and pulling his head down to hers. He kissed her, filling her with his tongue and his body with exquisitely matched motions. Calder settled against her and acted as if he had all the time in the world to make love to a woman in his kitchen, but Lisette had other ideas. She urged him closer, faster, until she climaxed almost immediately and, instead of being satisfied, Lisette wanted more.

She felt him grow larger in response to her own arousal. He plunged harder inside of her, and she opened her thighs wide to allow him freedom to move that wonderful body any way he wanted. He was hot and hard and all hers, at least for the moment, and Lisette forgot where she was and who she was and knew only that her body had missed making love and giving pleasure.

He stiffened and moved deep within her, and he groaned as his orgasm shook him. Lisette responded with another surprising climax of her own, one so deep and strong she wondered at the rancher's skill. Her hands found his sides and swept to his arched spine. Heaven, she thought, was—

"What the *hell*—" Calder withdrew from her body so quickly that Lisette wondered if the kitchen was on fire.

"What's wrong?"

"It broke," he groaned. "That's never happened before."

"What broke?" She hoped it was his penis and not the condom.

"The condom." He rolled away and grabbed his underwear. She saw he had very large, very white, very muscular thighs.

"Please tell me you're joking."

"Sweetheart, please tell me you're on the Pill or something."

"No," she said, reaching for her own clothes. It occurred to her, with a nauseating flip of her stomach, that she had just participated in what was known as "unsafe sex."

Not to mention she'd been half under a kitchen table with a stranger while doing so.

"Tell me you don't have any diseases," she begged. "And tell the truth." She managed to pull on her bra and tank top before he answered.

"Believe it or not, I've always used a condom. Always. No exceptions." She glanced over her shoulder to see that he was putting his shirt on and his jeans, though on, remained unzipped.

"Thank goodness," Lisette said.

"And you?"

"I've been tested. And I haven't had, um, sex in years." She finished dressing before she looked at him again. "I'm sorry," she said. "This whole thing was a mistake."

"No," the man said, a wry smile on his handsome face. "Not all of it, just the ending. That's pretty damn scary."

Lisette refused to think of it. She would go home and take a bath and trust that fate wouldn't play such a dirty trick on her just when she'd found a new life in Bliss. She grabbed her coat and, jamming the rest of her possessions into her tote bag, hurried out of Calder Brown's house.

If he said 'goodbye,' she didn't hear it.

4

"The more I see of men, the more I like dogs."
—Madame de Staël (1766-1817)

CAL SLEPT THAT NIGHT because he drank enough whiskey to drop a lesser man to the dirty floor of the Wedding Bell Blues bar. Mac saw that he got home by making sure that Jeb, one of the hands who never drank more than one light beer, drove his truck and shoved him through his bedroom door. He managed to fall over backward onto his four-poster log bed.

Still, even almost unconscious, he remembered how it felt to be inside Lisette, and how tight and warm she'd been, and the sounds she made when he moved inside of her. He got hard just remembering, even as drunk as he had been at two a.m. and even while the room spun around every time he opened his eyes. He liked to remember what happened on his kitchen floor, right up to the part when modern science let him down. When he got to that part, he tended to get a little tense and start swearing very loud, something that made his brain pound against the inside of his skull.

Truth was, when he woke Saturday morning it was to the immediate realization that he'd never had better sex, brief though it was. He closed his eyes against the sunlight that came straight through his windows to inflict pain. He thought of cold-sheets-winter-night sex with Lisette, imagined outdoors-by-the-river sweaty summer sex, whiskey-by-firelight sex, tongue sex, shower sex, against-the-wall sex and anything-while-Lisette-wore-black-lace sex. He discarded the thought of truck sex—he couldn't picture the elegant Frenchwoman sprawled half-naked in the front seat of his truck—but considered weekend-in-Las-Vegas sex, with Lisette in one of those skinny black dresses women wore to torture men, with high heels.

His body came painfully to life, so Calder forced himself to remember condom-breaking sex, a memory just as effective as a cold shower.

He didn't know what to do about that fiasco. Before the days of safe sex, a faulty condom meant several weeks of worrying if a sperm met the egg and a man met his fate by walking down the aisle with a gold ring in his pocket. But surely that kind of crap only happened to teenagers. It was too much to hope that either he or Lisette Hart was sterile, Calder supposed.

Cal forced himself to sit up and put both feet on the floor. He'd get himself cleaned up and then he'd head into town, get some breakfast and maybe even a haircut. He probably owed Lisette an apology, though it wasn't his fault the damn condom broke. But he should at least have walked her to her van when their kitchen-party sex was over. He should have kissed her goodbye and muttered the usual, "I'll call you."

He scratched at his chest for a moment, just to help with the thinking process.

And then he gave up. Thinking about last night was too damn hard. Within the last twelve hours or so, life had gotten a hell of a lot more complicated. He wished his right knee didn't ache. Next time he and Lisette would have sex in a bed.

"I'M AMAZED at the crowd." Ella turned her head to scan the dining room of the bowling alley, a favorite breakfast spot for the local residents of Bliss. "We have a very large number of tourists this weekend."

"And wait 'til *next* weekend," Grace warned. "The last weekend of the festival is traditionally a record-breaker."

Louisa stirred her coffee for what Ella decided

was the hundredth time. "Cam wasn't at the square dance last night. Said his back was bothering him."

"That's too bad, dear." Missy patted her friend's plump arm. "I'm sure he'll be at the ham and bean supper at the church tonight, though. No one ever misses that."

"No one over sixty," Ella declared. "The young folks are elsewhere." She wanted to add "Thank goodness," but didn't want to appear crabby. Just this morning Louisa had accused her of turning into an old crank. Ella wanted to make a conscious effort to be more cheerful, because she disliked her serious attitude towards matchmaking to be misinterpreted.

"Speaking of young folks," Grace said. "Has anyone come up with a match for Calder?"

The other three shook their heads. It wasn't often that the Saturday morning breakfast meeting of the Hearts Club lapsed into silence, but finding a bride for Calder Brown tended to stymie all four women.

"Oh, dear." Louisa gave her sister a worried look. "Do you think we've overreached? Perhaps we should think about Gabe O'Connor instead. I think we all have ideas in *that* direction, don't we?"

"Let's not get ahead of ourselves." The waitress hurried over and deposited their breakfasts, refilled their coffee and was gone before Ella could say any-

thing more than "thank you" to her. "We need to focus all of our energy on one subject. Look how well
that has worked in the past."

"Uh-oh." Louisa, seated across from her sister,
had a direct view of the entrance to the dining room.
It was clear she didn't like what she saw.

"What?"

"You're not going to like this," her sister said, and
Missy looked up from her blueberry pancakes to
agree.

"Don't look, Ella, and maybe he'll go away."

"Who?" She turned to look and saw Mac Brown
heading in their direction. Surely he wouldn't stop,
not after what happened so many years ago. They'd
managed to avoid each other for more years than
Ella cared to remember, despite both families having been in Bliss since the town didn't even have a
name. Mac was known for holding a grudge,
though Ella didn't blame him. She respected a good
grudge, had been known to hold a few herself, but
the sight of Mac irritated her nonetheless.

"He's probably coming over to tell us to mind our
own business," said Grace, calmly cutting up her
French toast. "He's a perfectly nice man when he
isn't all riled up."

"You do have that effect on him, Ella." Missy took

a bite of her pancake and sighed with pleasure. "Maybe you should—"

"Morning, ladies," Mac Brown said, pausing at the end of the booth they were crammed into. "Nice day."

Ella nodded, though the wind chill was fifteen and the sky looked grayer than her charcoal colored wool coat. "Good morning."

He took off his hat, exposing sparse white hair and a tanned head that matched the color of his face. Anyone would guess he was a rancher, from the sheepskin lined jacket to the Wrangler jeans and well-polished boots. He stood slightly bowlegged, too, as if he was just killing time before getting back on a horse. "May I have a word?"

"Of course," Louisa answered.

"About what?" Ella snapped, then wished she hadn't because her sister gave her one of those looks that said "you cranky old bat." "I mean," she said, using a much more conciliatory tone. "What can we do for you this morning, Mac?"

He gave her a sharp look, but he grabbed an empty chair from the table behind him as the people stood up to leave. Then he pushed it into position at the head of the ladies' table and sat down. "I have a dilemma."

They waited, though Missy continued to eat as if

she hadn't seen food for a week and Grace lifted her coffee cup hoping to catch the waitress's attention and get another refill.

"A matchmaking dilemma," he said, looking at Ella as if she was going to throw him out of the restaurant.

"Well, spit it out," she said. "We haven't got all day." Although they had. At least until five, when it was time to preside at the church supper. Ella personally basted the hams.

"I understand my grandson came to see you."

"He's at the top of our list this year," Louisa said. "He really should settle down, don't you think?"

"With all my heart." He smiled then, reminding Ella exactly how handsome Mac had been when he was younger. When they were all younger. "Do you have any one in mind for him?"

"We're still debating," Ella said. "We want to make the right decision."

"Meaning you haven't come up with anyone," Mac said. "It's not easy finding a woman for Calder, not when he's, uh, dated so many of the girls in town. But I have an idea."

"Really," Ella said, having forgotten all about her one scrambled egg and two slices of extra-crunchy bacon with a side of lightly buttered wheat toast.

"And precisely who is the lady who is the focus of your idea?"

"Ella, it's a damn good thing that fancy talking of yours doesn't make me get up and head home," the old man grumbled. The waitress brought him a cup of coffee and refilled Grace's cup before plopping a menu in front of Mac.

"Take your time, Mr. Brown," she said. "I can see you're enjoying the company."

Ella didn't appreciate the humor. Enjoying the company? Anyone could see this was strictly business. "Come, Mac, don't keep us in suspense. Unless you're playing one of your little jokes."

"This ain't no joke, Ella." He poured half a pitcher of cream in his coffee before answering the question they all wanted to know. "Lisette Hart. That's the one."

"Who on earth is Lisette Hart?"

"You're slipping, Ella," the old rancher said. "Thought you knew everyone in town."

"I'm not *slipping*," she retorted. "We've had quite a few new members to our community lately. Who is she?"

"The baker," Missy answered, dabbing her mouth with a paper napkin. "She's the one who bought the Dudleys' business."

"Ah, the Frenchwoman," Ella said with a nod. "I think I've seen her. Long, dark hair. Very pretty?"

"Yep." Mac nodded and took a big gulp of coffee. "The future mother of my great-grandchildren, that's her."

"How do you know she's the one?" Louisa pushed her empty plate aside and leaned forward. "Has something happened?"

"I think so." He cleared his throat before continuing, and Ella could swear the man blushed, but then again, the room was extremely warm. "She catered a party out at the ranch last night."

"Oh, how nice," Missy said. "What did she make?"

"Some kind of special chili, plus a bunch of other stuff. And a cake, too, with some kind of fancy fillin'. I had some for breakfast and it was real good this mornin', too," Mac said. "The woman cooks like a dream."

"You should taste her pies," Missy said. "Especially the custard."

"And her apple tarts." Grace, a retired home economics teacher, had a healthy respect for anyone who could make a decent tart. "You'd swear you were in Paris."

"Back to the subject," Ella said. "You think your grandson was attracted to this woman?"

Once again, Mac turned red from the top of his head to his nose. "I have reason to believe that, yes, Ella, I do."

"And you want us to do what, precisely?"

"Help matters along."

"Hmmm." Ella wasn't about to let on that this information came at a time when they were desperate for ideas. Letting Mac Brown know he'd actually rescued them from a very likely defeat was not something she wanted to do. "What do you know about her?"

"She's divorced. She has two little girls. And my grandson was uh, very taken with her last night."

"Your grandson has a reputation for being taken with anyone in a skirt, Mac. What makes this Mrs. Hart special?" She pulled a notebook and pen out of her purse while the old man thought about the question. Ella was prepared to wait for as long as it took. After all, a clue was a clue and help was help, even if it came from an untrustworthy and womanizing family like the Browns.

"Well," Mac said, taking another sip of coffee while he stalled for an answer. Ella sat, her pen poised over the paper. "At first she didn't seem real impressed with him."

Ella wrote down, "Smart."

"And he even went out to the kitchen a few times

to try to help out. Then he didn't come to, uh, the bar with the rest of the fellas last night, not until later. He wanted to be with her, I just know it."

"That's unusual?"

"Well, he sure was acting funny this morning," Mac said, frowning a little. "I think she got under his skin."

Ella put down a question mark. "This isn't much to go on," she said, "but it's a start."

"That's it?" He didn't look too happy.

"Unless you have anything else to add."

He frowned at the pad and then at Ella. "Not right now. I kinda wanted to be part of this. You know, help and all."

Louisa patted his gnarled hand. "We'll do the rest, Mac. And we'll let you know if we need anything."

"Yes," Ella sniffed, stuffing her notebook into her purse. "Don't call us. We'll call you."

Realizing he'd been dismissed, the rancher stood and dropped a couple of dollars on the table. "For the coffee," he muttered, before jamming his hat on his head and heading toward the door.

"Well, well," Ella said, not feeling the least bit cranky any longer. "How about that? Mac Brown asking for our help."

"You needn't gloat," Louisa said. "It's not the least bit attractive."

"Calder Brown and Lisette Hart," Grace murmured. "What do we think?"

"It's worth a try," Missy said.

"Yes." Louisa eyed her sister. "Ella?"

"Very satisfactory," she declared. "Mac Brown was begging for our help. I wish I could have taken a picture."

"But what about Lisette and Calder?"

"I'm willing to work on it," Ella said. "Men are idiots, for the most part, but old Mac might be on to something."

Louisa frowned at her. "There was a time you didn't think Mac Brown was such a fool. In fact—"

"Water under the bridge or over the dam, whatever. Today is my treat." Ella smiled once again and picked up the bill the waitress dropped on their table. No one could call her an old crank now.

"FROM NOW ON I will be a virtuous woman," Lisette promised herself. She spoke to the tray of cinnamon buns she was in the process of frosting because luckily there was no one to hear. Cosette and Amie, busy with an art project, were seated out front. Mona worked the register and served the customers while Lisette baked. She'd been awake since four, not that she'd slept very well. A guilty conscience made her toss under the quilts and even shed a few tears of mortification.

She would be able to rest soon, perhaps tiptoe upstairs for a brief rest while Mona handled the customers and poured coffee. The busy hours were behind them now. There might be a small lunch crowd on Saturday, but most of the customers would be tourists. They would stop in this afternoon for hot coffee and pastry while they warmed their hands. Some of the locals might pick up cakes or pies to take to a Saturday night gathering.

"I will never, ever talk to a cowboy again," she told the rolls. "Last night was a...fluke, a mistake, an error in judgment."

The accident that had occurred was another huge problem, but what were the chances that she would get pregnant from one sexual mistake? *High*, the voice inside her answered. She had never been one of those women who had to struggle to conceive. It was closer to, "I think I'll have a baby" and presto—it was done. Fertile Myrtle, her so-called husband had called her.

But she was older now. The girls were six and four. And Lisette was almost twenty-nine and nearing the end of her peak childbearing years. Her mother and grandmothers had all had their children while they were in their twenties. It was a family tradition, and one Lisette had had no quarrel with.

No, she'd had enough bad luck for a while. There would be no repercussions from last night, she was sure. The rancher would leave her alone—she'd heard he was a real heartbreaker—and she would consider herself the luckiest of women if she never had to lay eyes on him again.

"Lisette," Mona called, sticking her head into the kitchen. "There's a man here to see you."

She froze, letting the frosting mound on a corner roll in an unattractive puddle. "Who is it?" *Please, don't let it be him. He's seen me naked. I can't bear it.*

"Calder Brown," the girl whispered. "He said it's important."

"Tell him I'm busy. With a soufflé."

"Are you sure?"

Lisette imitated her grandmother when Mamere had had a difficult day and would brook no nonsense from anyone. *"Mais, oui."* Mona looked blank, so Lisette tried again. "Of course," she said, her smile grim. "Please explain that I am very busy here and will have to talk to him some other time."

"If you say so." Mona released the door to swing shut, leaving Lisette to debate drowning herself in her industrial-size sink.

He would go away. A man like that would not

stand around, his hat in his hand, waiting for a woman to have time for him.

No, she discovered ten minutes later, when she brought out the fresh tray of cinnamon rolls. A man like that would order a large cup of black coffee and sit down with two little girls and talk to them while they colored dancing turkeys red and orange.

"I've been learning all about you," he had the nerve to say when he looked up to see her staring at him.

"I see." She smoothed her hands along the sides of her old-fashioned apron, preferring faded calico and blue jeans to the chef's clothes she wore for catering.

"Can I take my break?" Mona asked, grabbing her jacket.

"Of course." The fewer witnesses the better. She didn't want everyone in town gossiping about the baker and the rancher.

"Mommy," Amie called. "Come see what we've made!"

"Turkeys," her older sister added. "For the Thanksgiving decorations." Lisette approached the table where the three of them sat. Her beautiful daughters, with their long dark hair and green eyes, could have been mistaken for twins if Cosette wasn't three inches taller than her younger sister.

"Wonderful," Lisette said. "We'll put some of them in the shop window for the holidays."

"Good morning," the rancher said, standing to greet her. "The girls and I were just getting acquainted."

"I see." He looked tired and a little pale, but those eyes still twinkled at her as if they shared a secret joke. The problem was that last night wasn't funny, or something she wanted to remember with laughter. Lisette's stomach did a nervous flip. "What can I do for you today, Mr. Brown?"

"We, uh, forgot to settle up last night." He reached into his jacket pocket and pulled out a checkbook. "I came by to pay for the party. Did you find the bill?"

"Yes." The bill, the one she had started to search for when she knocked her bag off the table and ended up naked, had been found in her papers before she went to bed last night and tucked next to the cash register this morning. "I'll get it for you."

He followed her, of course. She wasn't lucky enough to have the man stay in one place, pay his bill and then disappear. No, he would have to limp across the room and stand too close while she retrieved the bill.

"You're hurt," she said, handing him the paper.

"It's an old knee injury that flares up sometimes."

He glanced at the paper, then leaned on the glass covering the top of the pastry display to write out his check. Lisette had the uncomfortable feeling she knew exactly how he'd hurt his knee. Those ceramic tiles had to have been hard on a man's kneecaps. She blushed, and he shot her a questioning look when he handed her the check. She glanced down at the payment, which was one hundred dollars too high. Lisette attempted to hand it back to him.

"You've written this for the wrong amount," she said.

"Tip's included," he said, but he wasn't looking at her. And he wasn't taking the check back. His attention was on the tray of cinnamon rolls. "Boy, do those smell good."

"You are not going to tip me for last night," she said, wanting to cry. It was bad enough to behave like an insane, sexually-deprived woman and have sex with a stranger, but it was even worse to have the man want to *pay* her for it.

"Could I have a dozen of those?"

"Take it back," Lisette said. She tore the check in half and set the two pieces onto the glass above the rolls. "You've embarrassed me enough."

"What?" That caught his attention, because he had a genuinely bewildered expression on his handsome face. She wondered if he practiced it in front of the mirror.

"Write it again," she demanded. "With no tip."

"The cake woman always gets a tip." Then the problem seemed to dawn on him, because he went still. "Oh, sweetheart, you don't think—"

"Please don't call me that."

"Yes, ma'am." He pulled his checkbook out of his pocket once again and wrote another check. He handed the new one to her and waited while she checked to make sure the amount was right. "I never meant to insult you," he said, keeping his voice low.

"And I never meant for last night to happen," Lisette confessed. She glanced over to her daughters, who were watching curiously while their mother argued with a customer.

"I don't expect you to believe me, but I really don't know what happened," she said, turning to look into those hazel eyes that really were the most amazing color. "I mean, I know what *happened*," she stammered, "but it wasn't something I do. Not with strangers. Well, not with anyone. I mean, I was married, but—" She stopped, knowing she was making it worse. She could tell by the way the damn man started to smile.

"Do you have a black dress?" He leaned closer to

her, close enough that she could smell pine-scented soap and the faint aroma of leather.

"Why?"

"We're going out to dinner tonight."

"No, we're not." She realized she liked that leathery scent. Did all the men in Montana smell that good?

"Why not?"

"I have plans." That much was true. She wouldn't have gone out with Calder anyway, because he would naturally assume that their date would end in sex and she wasn't making that mistake again. Just the thought of another broken condom was enough to keep her virtuous for the rest of her unmarried life.

"With who?" Even when he glared at her he was a fine-looking man. She really wished he would grow a wart on his nose or lose a few teeth. And she wished he smelled like skunk. Any little deterrent would help her struggle with her attraction to him.

"That's none of your business," Lisette told him, but when he positively glowered at her she thought she'd put him out of his misery. "The girls and I have tickets to the church supper."

"Well, then," he drawled, putting his hat on. "I guess you don't want to drive to Bozeman for a steak and some heavy-duty dancing."

Bozeman was hours away, but somehow Lisette knew Calder wasn't joking. "No, thank you. I don't date."

His eyebrows rose and he looked at her with some disbelief. "Is that so? Then what was last night?"

"A mistake, Mr. Brown, that's all."

The man smiled, a lethally charming smile. "You'll get no argument from me. In fact, I came to apologize."

"For what?"

"About last night," he said.

"I'd like to forget about last night, if you don't mind."

He looked as if he wanted to say something, but changed his mind. "In that case, Mrs. Hart, give me a dozen of those cinnamon buns and I'll be on my way."

5

*"Obstacles usually stimulate passion, but some-
times they kill it."*
—*George Sand (1803-1876)*

"I SEE YOU'VE BEEN to the bakery." Mac eyed the box
Cal set in front of him on the kitchen table. "I
thought you'd sleep all day."

"I wanted to pay what we owed for last night."
He helped himself to a cup of coffee before he took
off his jacket, then reached into the cupboard for the
aspirin bottle. Between his hangover and his knee,
he wasn't having a real great Saturday.

"And the lady?"

"Mrs. Hart?" He swallowed three aspirin,
washed them down with hot coffee and tried not to
limp when he crossed over to the kitchen table and
sank into a chair across from his grandfather.

"Yes. How was Mrs. Hart?"

"Just fine and dandy." And about as cold-
blooded as a woman could be. He didn't understand why she'd turn down a fancy dinner in Boze-

man for a church supper in Bliss. There would be too many tourists and senior citizens there, too many families and too many green bean casseroles and meatloaves.

"I guess you were up to no good last night," the old man announced. He opened the lid on the box and inhaled. "My God, that woman can bake, can't she?"

"Help yourself, you old grump. Why don't you just come out and tell me what you're so ticked about?" He shrugged off his jacket and took another swallow of coffee. A nap would be good, and a couple of ice packs, too. Maybe he'd feel human by tonight and ready to go out and find a woman who actually liked him.

"I worry about you. You're limping," Mac said. "And you drink too much."

"It was Friday night," Cal tried to explain, though he knew it wasn't much of an excuse. Lately he'd been drinking because he was bored and ever since he'd turned thirty, one shot of whiskey could give him a hangover. It wasn't worth the trouble any longer, he supposed, but he didn't expect Mac to believe him. "I don't intend to hurt myself like that again."

"I'd like to believe that," he said. Cal watched his grandfather polish off one of those buns in four bites and then reach into the box for another. "I'd like to see you settle down, of course."

"So you've said."

"I also said to leave Mrs. Hart alone."

Cal decided this was a good time to stuff part of a cinnamon bun in his mouth. He nodded, though, to show the old man he agreed that it would be a good idea. After he swallowed, he said, "You won't get an argument from me."

"Too late," Mac said, scowling at him. "I went to see Ella Bliss today."

Cal choked, managing to catch his breath while his grandfather sat there and gave him a stare that could only be called unsympathetic. "I hope you're going to tell me you're the one looking for a wife. Is Ella interested in you or is it the other way around?"

Mac flushed, but he managed to grab another cinnamon roll and lick frosting off his thumb. "She and her sister, along with the Whitlow woman and Missy Perkins are going to get you a bride. And I think Mrs. Hart will do just fine."

The throbbing in his temples increased, which was probably why he wasn't thinking clearly. "Geez, Mac, I'm not getting married. And especially not to Lisette Hart." Just because he was still fantasizing about kitchen sex with the woman didn't mean he was going to go crazy and commit to a lifetime of love-on-the-tile-floor. Cal took another gulp of coffee to settle his suddenly queasy stomach. "I barely know the woman."

"You left your underwear under the table last night."

"What?" Cal wanted to look, but he resisted. Knowing his grandfather, the old man would probably wave them on a stick at any minute.

"So I'd say you know the woman pretty well already." Mac wiped his mouth with the back of his hand. "Unless you've started prancing around the house naked as the day you were born."

There wasn't much he could say, so Cal figured keeping his mouth shut was the smartest thing he could do, but the longer Mac glared at him the harder it became to stay silent. "I weakened," he admitted. "She hit me with a sponge and one thing led to another."

"St. Peter's church supper is tonight. You're going to give away the door prize."

"Mac—"

"You're going to act like the gentleman I know you can be and if the Hart woman is there you're to treat her with respect and not like one of your over-eager weekend girlfriends."

"I'm not sure that's such a good idea." The plan actually had some merit. He would get to see Lisette again and get Mac off his back at the same time. Appearing as a respected member of the community might make the woman realize what she was missing out on. He leaned back in his chair and thought about the Frenchwoman's satiny thighs. "I don't think she likes me."

"She'll get used to you," Mac promised, reaching for another cinnamon bun. "I've got my mind made up. I want that woman in the family."

"MOMMA, there's the man," Cosette said, pointing to a tall rancher standing behind what looked like a raffle table.

It wasn't fair, Lisette decided. Here she'd thought she'd escaped the embarrassing memories of last night by coming to church—well, the basement, anyway—but no. Calder Brown, large as life and looking like the charming devil he was, stood selling tickets to something that looked like a saddle— or a dead animal. It was hard to see through the crowd and she certainly wasn't going to stand on her tiptoes and stare.

"Ah, yes," she told her daughter, holding tightly to the hands of both of her children. She had just deposited a huge platter of heart-shaped shortbread cookies, in honor of the festival, to a corner table. Lisette wrapped it in silvery cellophane and tied a poufy bow with wide silver ribbon. The ladies in charge of the dessert table used it as a centerpiece and thanked her profusely.

Amie tugged on her mother's hand. "What man?"

"The turkey man," her sister said, pointing toward Calder, though Lisette wondered how the child could see anyone through the crowd. "He's over there."

"Goodie. I've got a turkey in my pocket."

The girls tugged their mother toward the rancher's table, but Lisette was smarter—and stronger. And also more determined. "Let's go have something to eat," she told them, moving the children in the opposite direction. They skirted long tables topped with paper cloths and decorated with pinecone arrangements and fall flowers, stepped around metal folding chairs and gentlemen's canes, and found their way into the line of people headed for the buffet table. Lisette smelled ham and beans, saw people pass them with plates piled high with turkey, macaroni and cheese, salad and rolls.

"I'm hungry," Cosette announced.

Amie slipped her hand from her mother's. "Me, too."

"Me, too," a low voice said behind them, and Lisette was afraid she recognized its owner. She didn't turn around, hoping against hope that the man standing at her back wasn't Calder Brown, but the expressions of delight on the girls' faces told her differently.

"Mr. Brown!" they squealed, identical smiles on their almost-identical faces.

"Mr. Brown," Lisette murmured, not quite facing him. "What are you doing here?"

"Handing out the door prize," he said. "It's my civic duty."

"I thought you were dancing in Bozeman."

"Not without you, sweetheart."

"Shh. Someone could hear you and think—"

"Think what?"

"Never mind." When she looked straight at him, she could see from the twinkle in his eyes that he was remembering last night just as she was.

"Think we knew each other? Everyone in town knows each other." He looked as if he enjoyed teasing her very much. He looked like the type who enjoyed teasing, period.

"My mommy doesn't dance," Cosette informed him. "She's a baker."

Amie tugged on his hand. "I've got a turkey in my pocket. Wanta see?"

"Sure."

She pulled out a carefully folded purple-colored

paper from the pocket of her velvet jumper and handed it to the rancher. He carefully opened it to reveal a paper turkey with one foot missing.

"Very nice," Cal declared, sounding surprisingly impressed.

"It's for you."

"Well, thank you. Can I keep it?" She nodded, watching him to make sure he would take care of her artwork properly. But Cal folded it back the way it was and tucked it into the breast pocket of his white Western shirt.

Lisette didn't know what to say. She didn't want to like him, she really didn't, but there was something so appealing about the man that she began to wonder if disliking him would be impossible.

She noticed that everyone knew him because she saw old men nod their greetings to him, elderly ladies asked him about his mother, the woman serving mashed potatoes wanted to know if Mac was coming tonight, too.

"It's my turn tonight," he said. "Mac had work to do." But quietly, to Lisette, he whispered, "Mac's real happy at home, watching television and eating your leftover chili."

"There wasn't any," she said, holding her plate out for a helping of sliced, roasted turkey and stuffing.

"He set some aside before it hit the table. I think he had chili for lunch, too, after he ate four of those cinnamon rolls of yours."

"I'm glad he liked it." She didn't know what else to say to the man. Talking about last night wasn't something she enjoyed doing and Calder Brown knew it and, for some reason, found it amusing. She busied herself with helping the girls fill their plates, then once they were through the line, looked around for three empty chairs. She expected Calder to walk away and join any of the hundred people who seemed to know him, but he followed her to a half-empty table.

"What are you doing?"

"Eating." He held a chair out for her, but Lisette didn't sit down. She set her plate on the table so she could get the girls settled, unrolled their silverware from the napkins and made sure they were settled in their chairs before she turned back to her own. Calder still stood, waiting for her.

"Calder—"

"Oh, good," he said, pushing her chair in. "You've stopped calling me Mr. Brown. That's an improvement."

"What are you doing?" she tried asking again.

"Trying to charm you into liking me."

"I like you," she admitted, surprising herself by saying it aloud. "I'm embarrassed about last night."

"So am I."

"You are?"

"Well," he said. "Not really."

"Go away. Please."

"No."

"People are looking at us."

"The festival makes people mind other people's business— Oh, hell," he groaned, staring at someone past Lisette's shoulder.

Lisette turned to see what he was staring at with such dismay. Two elderly ladies, one plump and one thin, headed toward their table. "Who are they?"

Calder had gone pale. "You don't know?"

"No. What's the matter with them?"

Before he could answer the two women reached the table and sat down across from them. The shorter one was out of breath and fanned her plump bosom as she leaned back in the chair. "My goodness," she said. "What a crowd tonight!"

"Good evening," the other one said, giving Calder a pointed look. "Are you going to introduce us to your friend, Calder?"

"Yes, Miss Ella. I'd like you to meet Lisette Hart and her two daughters, Amie and Cosette. Lisette, these ladies are the Bliss sisters, Miss Ella and Miss Louisa."

"How nice to meet you," Lisette said. "I've read about you in the paper. You're in charge of the matchmaking festival."

"And you own the bakery now, dear?" Louisa smiled at the children. "With your two pretty helpers?"

"Yes." The girls gave her shy smiles and continued to eat their macaroni, their favorite food.

Ella leaned forward. "How are you enjoying our town, Mrs. Hart?"

"Please call me Lisette," she said. "And I like Bliss very much. People are keeping me busy, which is wonderful."

"It's the festival," Ella explained. "It's good for business."

"Is there really a lot of matchmaking going on or is that just a myth?"

Ella looked as if she was going to faint and Lisette heard Calder choke, so she assumed she had said something very wrong.

"It is no myth, my dear," Ella Bliss replied, and Louisa quivered with laughter. "It's very, very real. In fact, historically Bliss has—"

"We've had a lot of success over the years,"

Louisa interrupted. "Would you like us to find you a nice young man?"

Now it was Lisette's turn to feel faint. "No, thank you."

"Do you have something against marriage?" This question came from Miss Ella.

"No, of course not," she fibbed, but she had the eerie feeling that the elderly woman knew she wasn't telling the truth.

"Hmmmm," was all she said.

"We're so happy you picked Bliss to come to," Louisa said. "The bakery is so lovely with the changes you've made. And Missy Perkins—she's a member of our card club—raves about your pies. You're taking orders for Thanksgiving, I heard."

"Yes."

"The holidays will be here before we know it," Miss Louisa said. "What beautiful daughters you have, Lisette." She looked at Calder. "Have you come up with your list yet, dear? Time's a-wasting, you know."

"Miss Louisa, I told you—"

"Oh, you'll change your mind soon enough," the woman countered. "Won't he, Ella? As soon as you're through with your supper, Calder, let us introduce you around a bit. Missy Perkins has a cousin whose daughter teaches in—"

"As you see, I'm here with Mrs. Hart," Calder interrupted. He rested his arm along the back of Lisette's chair and touched her shoulder with his thumb. It was a little nudge, one that said *don't tell them any different*.

"Well, well," Ella murmured, then turned to her sister. "We'd best get our supper, then, though I don't think we'll run out of food anytime soon." She eyed Lisette again. "I basted the hams myself. Secret recipe."

"Those are the best kind," Lisette said, trying not to wriggle away from Cal's touch, but he spread his entire hand on her shoulder as if they were the most intimate of friends.

Lisette jumped at the flash of heat from his fingers, which sent a piece of ham flying off her fork and across the table. "Excuse me," was all she could think to say.

"Sweetheart," the rancher cooed, leaning closer. "Are you all right?"

"I'm fine."

"I keep forgetting how ticklish you are," he said. "My mistake."

She kicked sideways as hard as she dared and knew she'd affected him when she heard him grunt.

"He has a terrible memory," Lisette explained, trying to ignore the surprised expressions on the faces of the elderly ladies seated across from them. "I think perhaps it comes from being kicked in the head by too many cows."

"My goodness," Miss Louisa said. "That must have hurt terribly."

"I've had worse broken hearts," he replied. "Like right now, for instance, Mrs. Hart here refuses to go out with me and it's just tearing me up inside."

"My goodness," the plump lady said, but her sister eyed Lisette with grudging respect.

"Let's leave the young people to finish their dinner," Ella said. "And Calder, we're keeping an eye on you. We all know it's time you settled down."

"EXCELLENT," Ella declared, helping herself to a slice of ham from the gold-rimmed platter of Mother's she'd loaned to the church for this occasion. "We've thrown him off a bit."

"How did you like my question about his list?" Louisa took another roll and a dollop of butter to go with it. "Did you see the look on his face?"

"It was priceless," Ella agreed. Almost as good as his grandfather's expression when he had to come crawling to her for help. Mac Brown had groveled, and Ella still couldn't believe her good fortune. Not only had Mac asked—begged—for her help, but he'd given them the name of a woman for his grand-son to marry.

"Mrs. Hart was lovely. Very mature and beauti-ful, too. I think she's perfect for him."

"Perfect or not, she's the only possibility we have." None of the members of the Hearts Club had come up with a name. Ella couldn't imagine giving in to defeat, but she supposed there was a first time for everything. And now if the Hart-Brown pairing didn't work out, the blame could be deposited on Mac's doorstep. "I hope she has the sense to keep out of his bed. Men love a chase and she shouldn't make it too easy for him."

"We should go to her shop soon. I wonder if she serves jasmine tea."

"You can ask, I suppose. Or bring your own and ask for hot water."

"Some people don't like it when I do that," Lou confided. "You know how cranky people can get, as if I don't want to pay for a hot drink. I always pay."

"I know." Ella watched her sister pile coleslaw in the center of her plate. "Could you hurry up a bit, Lou? My ham's going to be bone cold by the time we sit down."

"You can go on ahead," she offered. "The mayor's wife—what's her name—is saving us seats, isn't she?"

"Yes."

Louisa looked over her shoulder toward the table that held their prey. "I might scoot back to Calder and Mrs. Hart and see how they're doing."

"You'll do nothing of the sort," Ella said. "We're going to sit at the head table and chat with the mayor. If you go waltzing off to Calder now, he'll get suspicious."

"I'm a good actress," Lou said. "I can give Mrs. Hart Mother's glaze recipe."

"She doesn't bake hams. She bakes pastries." And right now, as Ella watched, Mrs. Hart pushed away her uneaten dinner and leaned over to speak to one of her daughters. Calder's arm was still across her chair in that proprietary way that gave Ella hope for his future as a happily married man.

"Her little girls seemed adorable."

Ella turned away to see her sister reach for a dish of cherry jello topped with whipped cream. "Aren't you done yet?"

Lou smiled. "I am now. Point me toward the head table."

"Thank goodness."

"We don't have to give a speech tonight, do we?"

"Just a short one. Then we get to pull raffle numbers out of the box."

"I like doing that. Cameron's here somewhere,"

her sister said, looking around as they passed through the crowd. "He wanted to have dessert together."

"We're not here to find you a husband," Ella reminded her, heartily sick of Louisa's single-minded pursuit of a love life. Ever since this year's festival began, her sister had talked of almost nothing else but finding a man. At eighty-one, Ella figured Louisa was barking up a long-dead tree. Her sister also liked anything that had to do with food, prizes and children. Ella preferred public speaking, social events—preferably those spotlighting the historical development of the town by Bliss ancestors—and matchmaking.

She took matchmaking quite seriously, as any of her friends would agree. Besides, she thought, remembering her achievements over the years, there was nothing quite like the thrill of success.

6

*"There's never any point in telling
bad news in a hurry."*
—Honoré de Balzac (1799-1850)

CAL WISHED Lisette hadn't kicked him, not that it
was much of a kick, though it sent a few tremors toward his recuperating knee. It had surprised him
more than anything. The woman had a knack for
surprising him.

He shouldn't look at a woman with two little girls
next to her and be thinking about sex. He should be
alone with her, or her kids should be somewhere
else. Kids were fine, as long as they didn't interrupt
his plans for seduction.

Not that this was the best place to seduce the
lovely Frenchwoman. Not in the middle of the senior citizen version of *The Dating Game*. It was just
an excuse to eat a lot of ham and raise money for the
church's building fund. St. Peter's was one of those
town structures that had seen better days. Hell, he'd
give them a check for the new roof if he thought that

would let them all go home and leave him alone with Lisette. Instead the volunteers came by with carafes of coffee and tea balanced on trays piled high with cups and saucers. They interrupted his plans to talk to Lisette. He knew he would have thought of something to say to her at any second.

"Coffee, please," Lisette said, smiling at the woman who handed her a cup.

"Me, too, thanks." Cal took the cup offered to him and waited for the lady to fill it. "So you're raising money for a new roof?"

She nodded. "Last winter was pretty hard on the church," she explained. "We hope to have enough money to start the renovations next spring."

In other words, parishioners would be shoveling snow off the roof this winter and praying the framework wouldn't collapse under the weight. Lisette took a sip of her coffee and then quickly set her cup down.

"That bad?" he joked, knowing that she must be used to fancier coffee. But she didn't reply. Instead she pushed back her chair and stood. "You're not leaving already, are you?"

"The girls have to go to the bathroom."

"You'll come back?" He sounded pitiful, even to his own ears.

"Are you that afraid the matchmakers will get

you?" She didn't glance in his direction, but he noticed she looked kind of pale. He remembered Mac's satisfaction at sending Ella Bliss to engineer a match between him and Lisette and wondered what she'd say if she knew. He supposed there were worse women to marry, if he was ever going to marry.

Which he wasn't.

"Afraid of the Bliss sisters?" he echoed. "Hell, yes. Anyone in their right mind would be. Look at Owen—he met his future wife right in Miss Ella's living room. They'll get you, too, if you're not careful." He'd seen some of the older men eyeing her, all right. There weren't too many single men in their thirties or forties here, which was in his favor. No competition, unless she preferred really older men.

"I doubt that very much. Good night." She took her purse and her daughters' hands and left him alone to ponder his fate. He didn't think she was going to come back. One of the volunteers came by and piled their dirty dishes on a tray and wiped off the table, preparing it for the next round of diners and erasing the fact that Lisette had been there at all.

He thought of his own kitchen table and what had happened there last night and immediately got painfully hard. It didn't help that he could see Lisette move slowly across the room toward the back, where the restrooms were down a short hallway. She looked beautiful tonight in a black skirt, one of those long skirts that shouldn't have looked sexy but did anyway. It had a slit in the back that made him long to slide his hand through the opening and caress the backs of her knees.

She would probably kick him again if he tried it, he reminded himself. He had to think about something else other than sex or he wouldn't be able to stand up and do his duty awarding the door prize, an antique saddle that Mac swore belonged to Custer. How his grandfather knew that or got the saddle, Cal didn't know. But Mac had a whole outbuilding full of stuff like that and he was real fussy about who got inside to see it.

"Cal?" The mayor waved to get his attention, calling out his name in the booming voice that had gotten him elected seven times. Seemed most folks appreciated a man who didn't mumble when he made a speech.

Cal waved back and discreetly adjusted his pants. Maybe he'd lost his touch with women now that he was thirty. Lisette Hart was proof of that. She'd left him alone without so much as a look of regret or a hint about seeing him later or an invitation to come by some afternoon for a cup of coffee and one of those fancy pastries.

Well, that was that then. He stood and prepared to charm the room full of seniors, one of whom would be the lucky winner of one of Mac's historical treasures. There was nothing to do about Lisette except forget last night ever happened.

And never get his hopes up about ever doing it again.

SHE DIDN'T THINK this would happen to her, hadn't seriously considered that it was a possibility, but when the aroma of coffee turned her stomach at the first whiff Lisette suspected she might be in trouble. All she could think to do was run, simply excuse herself and take the girls and escape.

Getting as far away from Calder seemed the best solution to a potentially nauseating situation.

"I don't have to go," Cosette said, stalling in front of the bathroom door.

"I do," Lisette told her. "Come on. You can wash your hands."

"I have to go," Amie announced, jumping up and down a little. Lisette guided both girls inside of the large ladies' room and made sure Amie was safely into a booth and that Cosette didn't wash her hands with water that was too hot. Another woman came in with her small daughter, who turned out to be one of Cosette's friends from school.

"Hi," the blond woman said, smiling at Lisette. "I'm Maggie Moore, Lanie's mom."

"We're friends," Cosette said. "Remember I told you I have a friend who has a horse?"

"Yes," Lisette said, hurriedly drying her hands with a paper towel before shaking Maggie's. "It's nice to meet both of you."

"Cosette lives in a donut shop," the little girl informed her mother.

"I know," Maggie said. "We have to visit her one of these days, don't we?"

Amie appeared, washed her hands and stood shyly waiting for the girls to notice her, which Lanie did. "You look just like your sister."

"Uh-huh."

Lisette felt another wave of dizziness hit her, so she held onto the sink with her right hand and tried hard to pretend this wasn't happening.

"You look a little pale," Maggie said. She was about Lisette's age, with streaky blond hair and big blue eyes. She looked as if she spent lots of time outside, a natural beauty with the kind of figure better suited for popping out of cake than Lisette's. "Are you feeling okay?

"I'm not sure. I think I'm just a little tired." She hadn't had much sleep last night. And she'd been on her feet since four-thirty, she reminded herself.

There were lots of reasons to feel this way other than the one she feared. "It's been a long day."

"Do you run the bakery all by yourself?"

"I have a little help," she said. "But there are some days I wonder if it's enough."

"Come out to the ranch sometime when you have an afternoon off," Maggie offered. "I'll show you around and the girls can play."

"I'd like that," she said, and meant it. She instinctively liked the woman, which reminded her how much she missed her friends in Los Angeles. Leaving them had been the hardest part of moving away. She looked down at Maggie's little girl, a sturdy blonde wearing cowboy boots and a denim jumper. "And you should come see us at the bakery," she said. "I have special cookies for friends."

Lanie grinned, showing a space where her two front teeth were missing. "Cool."

"Way cool," Cosette agreed.

Amie stared at those boots as if she had never seen anything so wonderful until Lanie disappeared inside the booth, and then she bent to see them from under the door.

"Well, it was nice meeting you," Lisette told them. "We're going to head home."

"You're not staying for the raffles?"

"No." That meant watching Calder Brown, which

wasn't good for her health—physically or emotionally.

"Too bad. I think we're the youngest people here and I figured we could stick together. I saw you've met Calder already."

"I catered a party for him last night."

"He's a character," Maggie said, a hint of fond amusement in her voice. "And a bit of a flirt."

"Are you—"

Maggie's mouth dropped. "Oh, Lord, no! We practically grew up together. We're even distantly related." She smiled. "If there's anything you want to know about the man, give me a call."

Lisette didn't especially appreciate the relief she felt at hearing that news. It wasn't as if she was interested in the man, even if she was physically attracted to him. *Had* been physically attracted to him. "Thanks, but I think I know enough to stay away from him."

"Oh, don't do that! Everyone loves Cal. He's okay, really," she said. "He just hasn't settled down yet." Maggie eyed her as if she was still unconvinced that Lisette was okay. "Can I get you a drink of water or something?"

Lisette shook her head, then wished she hadn't. Once again the dizziness threatened to blacken her vision. "I guess I'm more tired than I thought I was."

"Mommy brought lots of cookies," Cosette announced.

"Baking cookies takes a lot of talent," Maggie said. "I have to stick to the easy stuff, like vegetables. I was on the potato-peeling committee tonight."

"Come on, girls," Lisette said, knowing that once she got a good night's sleep she would feel much better. Tomorrow morning she would drink all the coffee she liked and nothing terrible would happen. "It's time to go home."

"Call me anytime," Maggie offered, as Lanie came out of the stall and went over to the sink. Maggie turned on the water for her and helped her with the soap. "Are you okay to drive?"

"We walked. We live above the bakery," she explained, as Maggie handed her daughter a paper towel.

"Your house must smell wonderful all the time."

"Like cinnamon and coffee," Lisette said, smiling as she opened the door for all three little girls to troupe through. She hoped she would be able to smell the coffee tomorrow without wanting to throw up.

"YOU'RE HOME EARLY. How did it go?"

Cal expected his grandfather to ask him that question, but he didn't expect the old man to be waiting at the kitchen door to ask it the minute Cal walked inside. So he pretended Mac meant the raffle. "The saddle was a big hit. I'm not sure how much money the raffle raised, but it was a hell of a lot, considering it's as old as it is."

"It's an an-*tique,*" Mac said, closing the door behind Cal. He followed him over to the sink and watched as Cal poured himself a glass of water and swallowed three aspirin. "I want to know about Mrs. Hart. How'd *that* go?"

"Well," Calder drawled, pretending to think about it for a minute. His grandfather was taking this whole thing way too seriously. "We had dinner together. With her little girls."

Mac beamed, his tanned face crinkling into hundreds of wrinkles. "Well," he drawled, "you must have looked like a real family man, eating supper with the kids and all."

"Yes, sir," Cal agreed. "Every time I belched I excused myself. I tried not to talk with my mouth full or wipe my mouth on my sleeve too many times."

"Quit givin' an old man a hard time," Mac said, his grin fading a little. "You didn't really do any of that stuff, did you?"

"Nope. I was the model of respectability. But she left early and took the girls with her and now I'm going to bed. Alone." The prospect didn't sound too bad, Cal figured, which meant he was either really tired or getting old. "I'm real tired," he declared.

"Was Ella Bliss there with her sister?"

"Would she be anywhere else?" Cal grimaced. Miss Ella's speech about the art of matchmaking had gone on for nine minutes, which was nine minutes too long. "I had to sit through the history of Bliss before I gave away the saddle. You should have been there, not me."

"I had a little indigestion," Mac said, patting his chest. "Probably was better I stayed home after all."

"To eat a quart of chili and the rest of the cinnamon rolls." Cal undid his shirtfront buttons and tugged his shirt from the waistband of his dark slacks. He'd dressed up for nothing, since Lisette hadn't given him so much as one appreciative glance the entire time they'd been together.

"Who won the saddle?"

"Maggie." Who'd been as excited as if she'd won a lottery. She'd also refilled his coffee and told him he wasn't getting any younger. "I helped her get it in her truck."

"And Mrs. Hart? What about her?"

Cal edged toward the hall, hoping to make a getaway before the old man could get too excited. "I don't have anything to report. She's not real interested in me, Mac. I told you that already."

"She was interested last night," the old man grumbled, following Cal as he headed toward the bedroom wing. "You must have done something wrong."

Cal stopped and turned. He stopped short of poking his grandfather's chest with his pointed index finger. "Look, I don't want to talk about this anymore. I don't want to get married. And I don't want any more damn questions. Call off the old witches and leave me *alone*."

"I see what's going on here," his grandfather drawled. He didn't look at all fazed, which made Cal even more frustrated.

"What?"

"She's playing hard to get, that's all. That means you have to try harder, let her see your good side for a change."

Cal swore. And then swore again. Mac patted his arm and announced that he was going back to the living room to watch television. "You get a good night's sleep, son, and don't get too discouraged. You might want to watch that language of yours, too. Mrs. Hart won't appreciate that kind of talk in front of her girls."

Cal opened his mouth to respond, then shut it again. He should never have left Las Vegas. This was all Owen Chase's fault and tomorrow he would tell him so. Tomorrow he would round up Gabe and see what they could do that didn't involve young women and old matchmakers.

"I DON'T THINK that's possible," the nurse informed Lisette, who held the phone against her ear with one hand and an early response pregnancy kit in the other. She'd bought the damn thing at the drugstore, on the way home from the church supper last night. And here she sat upstairs in her tiny kitchen when she should have been downstairs in the bakery baking for her Sunday morning customers.

"Well, I hope it isn't," Lisette told the hot line expert she'd been connected to when she'd dialed the 800-number. "But I knew within twenty-four hours with my other two pregnancies. I know it sounds ridiculous."

"Not really," the woman said, her voice growing kinder. "You want ridiculous? You wouldn't believe some of the calls I've had. Have you been trying to conceive long?"

"Not at all," Lisette said, debating whether or not to mention the broken condom. "It was an accident."

"Maybe you're simply imagining the worst then," the woman replied. "Wait three days before your period is due and then take the test. That's the most accurate way to find out, besides going to your doctor, of course."

"Of course. But if I take the test now—"

"It will be inconclusive," she said. "You'd be throwing your money away and you would only have to do it again."

"I see." Lisette slipped the test kit back into the plastic shopping bag. "Thank you."

"You're very welcome. Take good care of yourself."

"I will." She replaced the receiver on its hook on the wall and folded the bag around the box so that its label wasn't visible.

She told herself she was worried about nothing. She told herself that just because her girls had been conceived in November didn't mean that another child would be. Broken condoms happened, unfortunately. A one-time mistake couldn't result in pregnancy. The odds were so much against such a thing happening that Lisette dared to open a bag of coffee beans and take a whiff.

Which, she decided later, from a horizontal position on her bed, had not been a good idea.

"I TELL YOU, I saw her, plain as the nose on my face."

Grace, Ella and Lou stared at Missy as if she'd grown another head. Sometimes Ella wished she would, especially right now, so that Ella could dismiss her revelation and hurry them down the street to the bakery.

"It's too cold for this discussion," Ella insisted, conscious of the wind that blew against the backs of her calves, despite the thick stockings she'd worn to church.

Grace shook her head. "Well, it couldn't be, you know, *his.*"

"Hah!" was Louisa's response. "Everyone knows Calder Brown works fast. She's been in town for a few months now, she catered that party up at his place Friday night, and now look."

"Look at what?" Ella asked, trying not to shiver.

"You don't buy one of those kits the morning after. Or two mornings after. I don't think they work that fast," Grace explained.

"Well, there's only one way to find out," Louisa said, stopping in front of the drugstore door.

"We couldn't possibly—"

"Why not? It's not as if anyone will think it's for one of us."

Ella knew she had to draw the line somewhere.

"We'll be the laughingstocks of town, four old ladies looking at a pregnancy kit."

"No one will see. Grace, you've got the best eyes. You read what it says and the rest of us will cover you up," Lou said.

"Like a human shield," Missy declared, leading them into the store.

"You watch too many movies, Missy."

"Well, I'm not much of a reader," she confessed. "And I do have a certain fondness for action movies. And Steven Segal's muscles."

"I prefer romances," Louisa said, sighing. "I'm a Mel Gibson fan and I thought he was so handsome in—"

"Could we get a move on?" Ella nudged them in the direction of the women's personal products aisle. "I don't want to spend all day in here."

"You just don't believe it, that's all," Lou muttered.

Ella found this whole topic very distasteful. Mrs. Hart should have known better than to buy such a personal product in such a small town.

"There," Missy said, pointing to the bottom shelf. "She picked up that one." She looked at Grace. "Go to it."

"They didn't have these kits in my day. You went to the doctor to make sure, but really, a woman knew without anyone telling her or making little sticks turn pink." Grace picked up one of the boxes and began to read.

"My goodness," Ella couldn't help saying. "What if it's not Calder's?"

"How fast does it work?" Lou leaned over Grace's shoulder.

"I'd say about ten or twelve days after the, um, intimate moment."

"Do you think she knew Calder ten or twelve days ago?"

Ella could see the writing on the wall. "Calder was in Las Vegas up until this past week."

"So it's not his," Lou said, echoing her sister's thoughts. "Now we have to think of someone else for him."

"Oh, Lord." Ella couldn't imagine trying to come up with another potential bride for the man. Oh, he was handsome and charming and he had a way with the ladies, but a husband? She'd seen *dogs* with more potential for lifetime devotion than that young rancher. "We'll have to start over."

Grace replaced the box on the shelf and straightened. "Don't look now, but Mac Brown just walked in."

"Where?"

"Antacids."

"Who's going to tell him the bad news?" Missy whispered. "I think he has his heart set on Mrs. Hart's cooking."

"He'll simply have to survive the disappointment," Ella said, straightening her shoulders. She wished she'd remembered to refresh her lipstick. Lately Lou had been making her wear it, along with a tinge of pink rouge on her cheeks and a little face powder.

"Poor man," Missy said. "Do you think he has anyone else in mind?"

"I guess we can skip our visit to the bakery now," Ella said. "There's no sense in wasting our time with Mrs. Hart."

"Maybe he'll fall in love with her anyway, even if she's having someone else's baby."

"Missy," Ella said. "Get a grip on yourself, please. I'm about to break a man's heart."

"You don't look too upset," Lou pointed out. "I think you're gloating again."

"Robert MacKenzie Brown always thought he knew everything," Ella said. "I guess he's in for a shock."

7

"Men argue, nature acts."
                    —*Voltaire (1694-1778)*

"FIND SOMEONE ELSE?" Mac frowned at her, which made Ella wish she could reach out and shake him. "What on earth do you mean, find someone else?"

"I don't know how I can make it clearer." This was going to take longer than Ella thought. At this rate the Hearts Club would miss breakfast.

"But she's the one I want."

"I don't think so," Ella hedged, unwilling to betray a lady's privacy. She didn't know Mrs. Hart, other than having been introduced to her last night, but it didn't seem at all polite to discuss the woman's personal business. And pregnancy kits were certainly in the category of personal business.

"Why not?" He stood there like one of the bulls he owned, blocking the aisle and ready to paw the ground. "She can cook. And Cal likes her. He likes her a *lot*."

"How much?"

"Huh?"

"How much does he like her? Are they are on, um, intimate terms?" Perhaps a hint was in order.

"For cripe's sake, Ella, what are you asking me?"

"You've dropped your medication," she pointed out, after the box he had held hit the linoleum floor.

"Aw, hell," Mac grumbled, and bent down to retrieve it. When he straightened, she saw his face was red. "You're beginning to make me sorry I started all this."

"I met her last night. They make a handsome couple, MacKenzie," she said, deciding to use his full name. She remembered his wife, the beautiful Julia, sweetly calling him by that name whenever she was ready to leave one of the church socials and head back to their ranch. "But the match might not be in the cards. Mrs. Hart may be involved with someone else."

"No." The stubborn old fool shook his head.

"Yes. I'm afraid—"

"You know something I don't," he said, taking one step forward. They were about the same height, because they stood nose to nose and glared at each other for long seconds. "Tell me, Ella."

There was no hope for it then. Ella tilted her head and whispered the details of Missy's drugstore sighting last night. Missy had been picking up her high blood pressure medication and had been delayed because there was some mix-up with her insurance card. So, she had spent time roaming the aisles of the drugstore where she saw Lisette Hart select and then purchase the pregnancy test.

It was a very long whisper. And when she was finished, Ella moved away from the burly rancher and looked him right in those blue eyes of his.

"It's our secret," she said. "And I only told you because I had no choice. I would have preferred not to gossip—"

"Since when?"

Ella ignored the rude comment. "Naturally your grandson shouldn't be encouraged to pursue a woman who is already...involved."

"Ah," he said, not looking as disappointed as she thought he would have. "I see." In fact, he reached out and shook Ella's gloved hand. "You're not so bad after all."

"Thank you, I suppose." High praise indeed, Ella thought, watching Mac walk out of the drugstore without paying for the box of antacids in his hand. She'd tell the pharmacist to put it on his account.

Leave it to a Brown to think he could get away with something like that.

CLOSED? Cal glared at the sign taped to the glass entrance to Lisette's store and considered breaking the door down. It would be so simple and effective and yet he didn't think she'd appreciate the mess. Women didn't like mess. And they didn't like the men who made it. He leaned forward and read that on Sundays the shop closed at noon. He looked at his watch and realized he was forty-seven minutes too late to find out the answer to his question: was he going to be a father?

He ignored the wind and the threat of new snow in the air. He peered through the window hoping to see any sign of activity in the shop, hoping to catch a glimpse of Lisette or her daughters so one of them would unlock the door and let him in.

When that didn't work out, he resorted to Plan B, which involved making his way around the block to the back of the building and its parking area. It didn't take long to locate the set of stairs that led to Lisette's second story apartment. Once he approached the door he heard music and the sound of little girls' giggles. He took a deep breath and knocked. He didn't have to wait long for Lisette to open the door.

"Calder?" She hesitated before opening the door wider to let him in. "What are you doing here?"

"I wanted to see you," he managed to say. She looked beautiful with her hair down. It curled past the shoulders of her green sweater and down her back. She wore jeans and fluffy pink bedroom slippers shaped like rabbits.

He removed his Stetson hat and made sure he wiped his feet on the mat before he entered the kitchen. It was a small space, which meant he stood close to Lisette until she backed up a couple of steps and invited him into a small living room where the girls played with dolls and a plate of half-eaten sugar cookies sat in the middle of the coffee table. She turned down the music, some classical no-words kind of song, from the corner stereo system.

"What can I do for you today, Mr. Brown?" She gestured toward a green leather armchair next to the stereo, so Cal sat down. He dropped his hat onto Cosette's head and made her laugh. Amie smiled shyly and came over with one of her dolls, so he reached out and tugged gently on the child's long braid of hair, which made her smile even wider.

"Are you going to color with us today?" Cosette asked, fixing the hat on her head so she could see.

"Maybe in a little while," he said. "I came to talk to your mother." He looked over at Lisette, who had curled up on an overstuffed sofa piled high with velvet pillows. He admired the plump doll Amie showed him, then heaved a sigh of relief when Lisette asked her daughters to get their art supplies and color at the kitchen table for a few minutes. When the children left, Lisette finally looked at him again.

"What do you want?" she asked, those dark green eyes completely unreadable.

"You left pretty fast last night. I, uh, wondered if you were feeling all right."

"I was tired," she explained. "The shop was busier than usual yesterday."

He got up and walked over to the couch, then sat down next to her where he could get a good look at her face. "Are you pregnant?"

She grew so pale he worried she was going to keel over. "What?"

"You heard me, Lisette. I'm trying to put two and two together here. And I came to get some answers."

"You're not going to get any," she said, keeping her voice low.

"This is a small town, sweetheart. You bought something at the drugstore last night that makes me wonder about the little accident we had Friday."

"You shouldn't buy cheap condoms," she whispered.

"They weren't cheap, just defective. And you shouldn't go advertising your personal life at the local drugstore."

"Advertising?" she squeaked. "What do you do? Have spies all over town?"

"Well, sort of." Mac certainly got around and the old man's excitement when he'd awakened him this morning had been something to see.

"I think you should leave now."

He shook his head. "No way. Did you buy that thing because you think you could be pregnant because of what happened Friday night?"

"Shhh," she hissed. "Don't say that word."

"What word?"

She lowered her voice. "Pregnant. My girls could hear you."

He moved closer to her, which she didn't protest. He wondered if she even noticed, because now she had closed her eyes and looked as if she wanted to be somewhere else.

"Could you tell me how this test kit works?"

"Aren't you a cattle rancher? Don't you know?"

"I'm asking you if you're pregnant."

"I don't have any idea."

"Then why did you buy the damn thing?"

Lisette opened her eyes and rested her head on her hand. "Each time I was pregnant with the girls I couldn't stand the smell of coffee."

He waited.

"Right away," she added. "Before tests and the visit to the doctor and the obvious biological signs."

"And now?" He hoped he wasn't going to hear what he thought he was going to hear, but this coffee thing sounded ominous.

"Last night at the church I tried to drink coffee and all of a sudden I didn't feel well."

"Oh, damn."

"Please. The girls."

"Sorry." Calder knew he was going to have to get better at behaving himself around women. "If this coffee theory of yours works out, does that mean I'm the father or could there be someone else?"

She took her time answering. "I'm afraid you're the only candidate."

He took another deep breath. So Mac was right after all and another generation of Browns might be in the works, microscopic as the future little cattle baron might be. "When will you know?"

"I can take the test in about ten days and most likely get an accurate reading," she said, finally turning to look at him. "But you don't have to worry about it."

"I don't?"

"No. Not in the least."

"You don't mean you'd have an abortion, do you?" He'd considered she might take that option, but he had decided no kid of his was going to be gotten rid of.

"No."

"Good. I figure we can work things out somehow," he said. He thought for a moment she was going to start crying. What the hell would he do then? He felt in his pocket to see if he had a handkerchief, but he couldn't feel it.

"Well," she said, "That's a relief."

"You don't have to be sarcastic," he murmured. He looked at her beautiful mouth and thought about kissing her. It might be worth a try, especially now that they were sitting next to each other on this comfortable sofa.

"Don't even think about it," she said, obviously able to read his mind. "That's what started all this in the first place."

"I can't help it if I'm hard to resist." He grinned at her to show her he was only kidding.

"Right now you're about as irresistible as a pot of Maxwell House dark roast."

Calder wasn't about to let himself get sidetracked by insults. He couldn't believe, especially after that brief time of extremely hot sex, that this woman actually was immune to him.

He knew women. And he was ready to get to know this particular woman a hell of a lot better.

"We'll get married," he heard himself say. He couldn't believe the words came out of his mouth, but he'd given the problem some thought on the drive in from the ranch. There were lots of possibilities, but now it narrowed down to one thing: if Lisette was pregnant with his child he would marry her. No child of his was going to grow up without the Brown name. Period.

"Mommy?" Cosette peered into the living room. "I'm hungry."

"Just a minute, honey." Lisette untangled her legs and began to leave the couch, but Cal put out his hand and touched her arm.

"I mean it, sweetheart."

"I'm not getting married," she said. "Whether I'm—pregnant or not. And I think it's way too soon to talk about this, so you should go home and do whatever it is you do on Sundays."

"I usually sleep late."

"Well, then," she said, getting off the couch. "You'd better go home and get started."

"And what about you?"

She pushed her hair back from her face and sighed. "What about me, Cal?"

"You look like you're the one who could use some sleep, not me."

"After I feed the girls, clean up the kitchen, go to

the laundromat, buy groceries and clean the house I'll be happy to lie down," she said, heading toward the kitchen. "Goodbye. Thanks for coming over."

"I'm serious," he insisted, following her. He liked the way her jeans curved so nicely around that shapely rear end. "Can't all that stuff wait?"

Lisette waved one hand toward the two little girls who kneeled on kitchen chairs and attempted to spread peanut butter and apricot jam on thick slabs of homemade bread. From the size of the holes in the bread and the globs of jam on the tabletop, it wasn't going real well. "Wait?" she asked. "I don't think so."

"You really don't look too good," he felt obligated to point out. "Are you sure you're not sick instead of, uh, the other thing? There must be a way to find out now, instead of waiting for ten days." If so, he had a lot of bachelor-type things to do in ten days.

"It would be easier to be sick," she agreed. "And a nice simple virus would save me about nineteen years of responsibility, so keep your fingers crossed."

"Go to bed," Cal insisted, lifting the jelly knife from Cosette's hand. "I'll make them lunch and pour milk and all that. Maybe we'll even go to the movies."

"The movies?" Cosette's eyes widened and Amie smiled. "What movie?"

"Yes," Lisette said, wrapping the bread securely with plastic wrap. "What movie?"

"The Sunday matinee used to be for kids," Cal said, realizing too late that he hadn't any idea what was playing. "We can walk down there and see if anything is, uh, G-rated."

"Why?" She had her hands on her hips now, as if she was ready for a fight.

"Because," he said, "I think you need taking care of."

Moments later, standing outside on the landing and looking at the door that had just closed in his face, Cal realized that probably had been the wrong thing to say.

IT WASN'T LIKE HER to be rude, but Lisette either had to kick him out or start sobbing like a baby, so she really didn't have much choice. Not if she wanted to keep her dignity.

Then she remembered popping out of a cake and making love to a cowboy on a tiled floor and decided that any dignity she possessed was certainly shot to pieces.

And crying about it wasn't going to get her work done or add to her children's emotional well-being, so Lisette decided to fix herself a cup of tea and go over the week's accounts. She also decided that she wasn't pregnant, and even if she was she would deal with it.

Without tears. Without regrets. And without the sexy rancher's help.

CAL WENT HOME and called Gabe, who had two kids and should know all about women knowing when they're pregnant, but Gabe only laughed and told him it was about time his shenanigans caught up with him.

"I don't remember the details," his old friend said, once he'd stopped laughing. "Who's the lucky lady?"

"None of your damn business," Cal said, but Gabe chuckled again and told him he'd be glad to teach him how to change diapers before Cal hung up the phone.

He tried getting hold of Owen, who'd had his youngest niece—a real, honest to goodness baby— to care for since his sister died, but Owen's wife answered the phone and said Owen was out in the horse barn. Cal thought he remembered this Suzanne woman was a writer, not a nurse, so he didn't bother to ask her what she knew about pregnancy kits and conception, even though he was so desperate that he was tempted. Owen would have his hide if Cal even asked, and Owen wasn't someone a man wanted to mess with.

Doc Hawley answered his phone, but said he'd have to check with the lab at the hospital to find out how accurate a blood test would be three days after intercourse. And Calder would just have to wait 'til halftime because Seattle was ahead by a field goal and everyone knew how seriously Doc followed the Seahawks team. And didn't Cal know better than to fool around without wearing a rubber?

Cal tried to explain, but Doc muttered something about a commercial being over and hung up. So Calder was no closer to finding the answer to the biological mystery of parenthood than he had been when he'd been kicked out of Lisette's apartment.

"Where is she?" Mac poked his head into Cal's office and glared at him. "I thought you were going to go to town and straighten all of this out."

"I tried." The last thing he needed was the old man getting personally involved. It was bad enough that Mac had had to wake him up with the news that he might be a daddy in nine months. His grandfather enjoyed meddling in his business and always had.

"And?" Mac stepped inside and made his way around piles of papers and magazines, account books and stacks of photographs before he settled himself in the chair in front of Cal's desk. "You should let Hetty in here to clean this place up."

"Never." Cal took his booted feet off the top of the desk and attempted to divert the questioning. "Lisette doesn't know anything yet. It takes at least a week or so, she said, before she can take the test. I called Doc Hawley to find out if there was any way to find out sooner, but he was watching the game."

"Find out how?"

Cal shrugged. "I don't know. Blood test, urine test, something. I'd sure as hell like to know that I'm off the hook."

"That's what you get for not using a condom like I taught you." Mac smiled to himself. "Still, it'd sure be nice to hear the pitter-patter of little feet around the ranch again. I sure can't be too mad at you."

"The condom broke." He leaned back in his chair and put his hands behind his head. "I didn't have a prayer in hell, 'cause I was in Miss Ella's and Miss Louisa's living room last week. They jinxed me, that's what they did."

"I'd say it was your lucky day," his grandfather replied. "Ella Bliss means well, though she's damn irritating most all the time. Always has been."

"I thought I understood women," Calder declared, "but Lisette doesn't want to have anything to do with me."

"You'll have to work harder at impressing her." Mac pointed to the phone. "Call her up and bring her out here for supper tonight. Those girls of hers can come, too."

"And what's this happy little family of ours going to eat?"

"I'll call Hetty and have her bring over something. She's always got casseroles and the like in the freezer."

"She'll say no. Not Hetty. Lisette."

"What happened to all that Calder Brown charm?"

"The woman's immune. She doesn't want anything to do with me, whether she's pregnant or not."

"You'd better change her mind, Cal. No great-grandson of mine is going to enter the world as anybody else but a Brown."

"I told her that already."

"You're not supposed to tell her the *truth*," Mac said. "You're supposed to tell her she's beautiful and you can't live without her."

"She'd never believe that, you know. She's smart."

"Not smart enough," Mac said. "Or she'd never have ended up on the kitchen floor with you."

8

"Curiosity plays an important part in love."
—*Stendhal (1783-1842)*

SHE REFUSED the rancher's dinner invitation, which shouldn't have come as any surprise. Lisette meant it when she said she had a lot to do. Before the phone rang she'd sat at her kitchen table going over the books wondering if there was a way to afford more help. She'd finally stopped obsessing over the calendar and worrying about what she would encounter in nine days when she took the test kit into the bathroom. She'd always wanted more children, but it wasn't going to be easy to have a baby and run a business at the same time.

"Your kids are invited, too," Cal said. "Mac said something about teaching them to ride?"

"Yes, but—"

"You can bring your laundry and do it here."

"I was going to say that I didn't think the girls could learn to ride horses in the middle of winter. Isn't it too cold?"

"We've got a pretty sheltered paddock, but I think all Mac had in mind was letting them meet a couple of horses and maybe sit on top of them in the barn."

"Horses?" Cosette appeared in the doorway, a Barbie doll clutched in her hand. "We're going to ride horses?"

Lisette shook her head and then spoke into the telephone. "Tell him I appreciate the offer, but we'll have to come out another time."

"We're going to ride horses? Say yes, Mommy!" Cosette hurried over and looked as if she'd like to take over the telephone and make the plans herself.

"How about tomorrow?" he asked.

"Stop it." She looked at her daughter when she spoke, but hoped Calder would obey, too.

He didn't. Instead he said, "You're closed on Mondays, I saw."

"I mean it, Calder. I want this to stop. And I want you to go away."

"I am away," he said, sounding amused. "I'm forty miles out of town."

"And I want you to stay there and leave me alone."

"For how long?"

Good question. A lifetime? 'Til the kid goes to college? "I'll call you in a couple of weeks."

"You can have a blood test on Friday."

"And suddenly you're an expert."

"I talked to a doctor. There's something called the HCG qualitative test which will give us a yes or a no."

"Why are you doing this?"

"Don't you want to know as soon as you can?"

She knew, but she hoped she didn't. But if she wasn't pregnant, then this man would leave her alone, would seduce someone else and do whatever handsome cowboys did all winter. She didn't want him in her life, didn't want any man in her life.

"The sooner the better," she agreed. "Though I don't understand why you are in such a hurry."

"I don't like problems hanging over my head."

"It isn't going to be your problem."

"Sweetheart, if you believe that then you're in for a surprise."

CALDER WAITED it out for three more days. Each day brought new ideas from Mac, suggestions that ranged from inviting the woman to dinner to out-and-out kidnapping. He didn't tell Mac that he went to the bakery each morning. Cosette was in kindergarten, but Amie would visit with him from her little table in the corner. Her mother would bring out a tray of something that smelled like heaven, look at him and sigh, then retreat back into her kitchen.

"A refill, Calder?" At least Mona spoke to him, once she'd gotten over her shyness.

"Sure. Maybe some of that French dark-roasted blend?"

"Okay." She returned with a fresh cup of coffee for him. "Mrs. H. will be out soon. I go on my break at ten."

He knew that, which was exactly why he sat here. Besides, he liked keeping Amie company. In three days they'd progressed from coloring turkeys to coloring horses. Today Cal brought a new coloring book, *Johnny Goes To The Rodeo* and his own set of crayons, the biggest box he could find at the drugstore. And, just to keep things interesting, he'd bought a set of markers that were supposed to sparkle. Any man with a working brain knew that females liked things that sparkled. Out of the corner of his eye he saw the kitchen door swing open and deposit Lisette behind the counter. She didn't stay there; in fact, she went around and headed in his direction. When she stopped at the table he thought he caught a whiff of apple pie.

"What are you doing?"

"Good morning to you, too." He winked at Amie

and handed her an orange crayon. "Try this on the bridle."

"Bridle?" She had her mother's frown. He pointed to the leather straps on the horse's head. "Right there."

"Join us?" He slid his coffee to the other side of him, away from the empty chair. "Are you still sick?"

"Only around coffee," she said, eyeing his cup with something that looked like pain.

"How do you survive serving it to customers?"

"I breathe through my mouth."

He took a piece of paper from his shirt pocket and set it in front of her. "It's for the blood test. From Doc Hawley. You can go to the clinic tomorrow and find out for sure."

"Thank you." She took the paper and studied it for a long moment before she spoke. "We certainly got ourselves into a mess."

"It was my fault," he said, but it was hard to work up any real sorrow. The more he thought about having a son the more he liked the idea.

Amie looked up from her coloring book. "You hafta say you're sorry," she told him.

He smiled. "I'm sorry," he fibbed. "I surely am."

"Could we not talk about this anymore?" Lisette

stood as the front door jangled and two elderly ladies entered the room.

"Have dinner with me," he urged. "All three of you." She'd refused before, but he figured she'd change her mind one of these times.

"Okay," Amie said, but Lisette didn't even hesitate.

"No, thank you."

"Mac wants to cook for you," Cal said, but he was talking to her back as she walked toward the counter. "He's an old man who could die at any time, so you might not want to wait much longer."

One of the customers turned to frown, sending him a look that Cal swore should have turned him to stone. Ella Bliss was not amused.

"Calder Brown, what kind of a joke is that?"

"Well, not a very—"

"Your dear mother raised you better than that. You should have more respect for your grandfather than to joke about his death." She frowned even more, making her look like an old vulture ready to swoop down on his frozen carcass. "You were joking, weren't you? MacKenzie isn't ill?"

"No, Miss Ella, he was fine when I saw him this morning."

Louisa waved to him. "How is your mother, Calder? Does she still like living in California?"

"She sure does," he replied, glad to change the subject from disrespect to San Diego.

"Will she be home for the holidays?"

"Yes, Miss Louisa, as far as I know." It dawned on him that he'd better make an honest woman out of Lisette by Thanksgiving or his mother would have his hide.

"May I help you ladies with something?" Lisette stood behind the counter now and looked as if she was trying not to laugh. He'd have to explain to her later that the Bliss sisters were not to be taken lightly.

"I'd love a cup of jasmine tea," Miss Louisa said, looking at the selection of tea bags displayed in a thick white bowl on the counter. "I'm so pleased to see you serve it now."

"I read all the suggestions in the suggestion box," Lisette answered. "I want to keep my customers happy."

"We don't have time for tea," Miss Ella declared. "Not today. We need desserts for our card party this afternoon. What do you suggest?"

Calder returned his attention to Amie, who appeared to want him to admire her latest creation. "I've always liked purple horses," he told her. "They run the fastest."

"Thank you," the little miniature of her mother said primly. "Me, too."

He should have known Miss Ella wouldn't mind her own business. He looked up to see the elderly woman peering at the coloring book. "Artwork, Calder? And with a child? Does this mean you're keeping company with Mrs. Hart?"

"Mrs. Hart won't have anything to do with me, Miss Ella." Calder smiled his most charming smile. "Do you have any suggestions to help me out?"

"I assume you're teasing me again." She leaned forward and lowered her voice. "Seriously, I don't think she's the right one for you, dear."

"Work with me, Miss Ella," Cal said, winking at her. "I could use all the help I can get."

But the elder Bliss sister rolled her eyes and hurried back to the counter to prevent her sister from purchasing an extra half-dozen cream puffs to go along with an assortment of fruit tarts and napoleons.

"She looks like a witch," Amie whispered.

"But she's not," Cal whispered back. "And even if she was, we wouldn't be scared, right?"

"Right." Amie flipped the pages of the coloring book until she found another page with horses on it. "You color good."

"Thanks. So do you."

"Do you have kids?"

"Nope." Not yet, but if he was going to be a father he was damn well going to be raising his child on the ranch where he belonged. Calder looked over at Lisette, who was busy boxing up pastries for her customers. She had yet to understand that Calder Brown always got his way.

"I'M TELLING YOU, Grace. We saw it with our own eyes." Ella did not understand why her word was doubted. Had she ever told a lie? Not likely, unless it was in the interest of matchmaking and then anything was fair and acceptable behavior.

"He was coloring? With a child?" Grace didn't seem convinced. She tossed the ace of clubs into the center of the table and took the trick. "Calder must have something up his sleeve."

"It's the baker," Louisa insisted. "He's in love with Mrs. Hart. What else could it be?"

Missy leaned forward. "But what about the you-know-what?"

"You don't have to whisper, Missy." Ella took another sip of coffee and returned the delicate china cup to its saucer. "We all know what you mean."

"Sorry. But doesn't this mean that we're done with Calder? If he has found someone he wants to marry, we can move on to someone else."

"Move on?" Ella didn't like the sound of that. "I'll believe Calder's marriage when and if I see the certificate itself. Besides, we don't know the details."

Louisa chuckled, her plump cheeks puffing out like tomatoes. "But we know who to ask, don't we?"

"Who?" Missy usually had trouble keeping up.

"Mac Brown, dear." Grace threw another card out, a low diamond. "Ella must call him."

"And ask what precisely?" Ella frowned. "If Mrs. Hart is carrying Calder's child? I don't see how that's possible."

"It's a tidy solution to finding the man a wife. Even you must admit that, Ella." Louisa played a card and then continued, "And if that's settled, we can talk about other matches."

"For instance?"

"Me. Cameron has been paying attention to me," she announced, as if that was news to anyone. "I'm debating about whether or not to get serious."

"Get serious?" Ella echoed. "Does that mean exchanging kisses on the sofa or picking out side-by-side burial plots?"

"It means intimacy," she answered.

Missy choked back her laughter. "I know you've decided to find romance, Lou, dear, but are you sure you know what you're getting into?"

"Could we discuss more important matters, such

as our next project? We have three more days until the festival ends," Grace said.

Ella wasn't prepared to rush into anything new. "We don't know that Calder will *marry* the woman."

"That's why you have to call Mac," Louisa said. "So we can move on."

"And ask him if his grandson is going to do the right thing by the baker? I don't see how I can question MacKenzie about such personal matters, I really don't." There were times when even the town's most successful matchmaker had to draw the line.

"He came to you first," Grace pointed out. "He asked for your help. Now you need to find out if you're still needed. If not, we can talk about Maggie."

"Maggie?" Louisa's mouth fell open. "Maggie *Moore?*"

Missy reached into her purse and pulled out a slip of violet paper. "I wrote down several names, too, and I thought—"

"She'll never let us help," Louisa interrupted. "You know how she is."

Ella held up her hand, which made the other three women stop talking and look at her.

"Just one moment," she said, still debating about

her phone call to Mac. "We will all think about what to do with Maggie at Saturday's breakfast."

"But what about Calder?" her sister asked.

"Let me see what I can find out," Ella answered. She would call Mac, chat about a donation to the library fund and then she would ask if he still needed her help. If he said no, then she would wait for him to thank her for her help. If he said yes, well, she would try not to act too pleased. She would even pretend to be tired of Calder Brown and his marital problems.

Sometimes a woman shouldn't act too eager.

"THIS HAS BEEN, I think the second worst week in my life." Then again, as Lisette frosted a small three-tier wedding cake for a reception at the Wedding Bell Blues that night, she remembered other really terrible weeks—her grandmother's death, the discovery she wasn't really married, the time Cosette nearly died from complications from chicken pox— so maybe this week should actually be ranked tenth or eleventh.

Maggie Moore, having brought Cosette home from playing with Lanie at the ranch, sat at the counter and watched the decorating process. "Why the second worst?"

"I'm not sure you'd believe it if I told you," Lisette said, carefully transferring a frosting rose to the border of the smallest circle, which would be the top tier when she assembled the cake later on.

"I was widowed four years ago," Maggie said. "I've had a few bad weeks myself."

"I'm sorry." She paused in her work and looked at her new friend. "That was thoughtless of me."

Maggie smiled. "You don't have to apologize. It wasn't exactly a marriage made in heaven."

"Contrary to Bliss tradition?"

"That's right," Maggie said. "And does this terrible week have anything to do with Calder?"

"I really don't like wedding cakes." Lisette tucked another rose onto the edge of the cake. "Or weddings."

"I'll take that as a yes," she said.

"Because I hate this cake?"

"That, and because Cosette said 'Mr. Brown' comes to the bakery every day and colors with Amie and he's promised to teach them to ride." Maggie's smile was sympathetic. "There aren't too many secrets in a small town."

"I'm pregnant." Lisette sat down on the stool and set her knife on a piece of wax paper. "I found out today."

"And this has something to do with Cal?"

"Yes." She refused to cry. There were worse

things than being pregnant, far worse things. She would make a list so she could remind herself often. "But would you please keep it to yourself?"

"Sure." Maggie reached over and put her hand on top of Lisette's for a moment and then withdrew. "You don't know me very well, but I swear I'm really great at keeping secrets."

"Thanks."

"So does he know?"

"He knows it's a possibility." And he would call tonight to find out if she had the blood test and what the results were. And once she told him he would insist on being part of her life.

"And then what?"

"I don't have any idea. You've known him a long time—"

"Almost my entire life," Maggie interjected. "He'll do the right thing."

"The right thing for whom?" Lisette asked. "I don't want another husband. A bad one is worse than none at all."

"Somehow I don't think Cal is going to understand. If you're carrying his baby I think he's going to want to be part of that child's life. The Browns take 'family' very seriously, Lisette."

"He's supposed to be a wild bachelor. I've heard about his reputation."

"Yes, the women love him and he loves women, but I don't think he's going to ignore his own child."

"I don't want a man—any man—in my life right now," Lisette said, wondering if she was telling the truth to her new friend and to herself. Something about Cal made her want to hold on and never let go. "They're too much trouble."

"You'll get no argument from me," her friend said, chuckling. "But Calder is going to have his own opinion about all of this."

"He can't make me marry him."

Maggie's eyebrows rose. "Make you? Maybe not, but don't let his cowboy talk fool you. He's wealthy and he's smart and he's used to getting his own way. But Lisette?"

"What?"

"He's a decent man. Don't toss him aside too soon." She paused, then asked, "Do your girls have a father?"

"Yes, but I have full custody." And their father was in prison, where he belonged. By the time he got out the girls would be in college.

"Then think about Cal," Maggie urged. "You could do worse."

Lisette picked up her knife and selected another frosting rose. "Yes," she said, "I know."

"Well?"

Cal put down the phone and shook his head. "They won't tell me. Said it's confidential."

"Shoot." Mac opened the refrigerator and pulled out two bottles of beer. He handed one to Cal and popped the lid off the other for himself. "Dang doctors."

"At least she had the test today, like I asked." He thought about drinking the beer, then he thought about heading into town. He looked at his watch. The bakery closed at four and she'd be upstairs with the girls fixing dinner right about now, if he guessed right.

"You going to the grange thing tonight?"

Cal shook his head. "Nah. I'm going to go find out if I'm going to be a father or not."

"I meant after that," Mac said. "You won't want to miss the chili cook-off. And the beer's a buck a glass."

"Sounds like a good time, all right," Cal said, grabbing his hat and coat. "I'll be there later if Lisette kicks me out."

Poor Mac looked like he was going to cry. "She's a damn fine woman, son. I hope she's the mother of my great-grandson."

"Try not to think about it too much," Cal said. "You get yourself too worked up."

"Can't help it," his grandfather said. "I keep thinking about you finally settling down and I just get my hopes up."

"Settling down? Me?" Cal grinned and took the beer with him. "See you later, old man."

"Don't forget to talk real sweet," Mac called after him, which made Cal grin. Lisette wasn't much for sweet talk. She was outspoken and funny, sexy and shy, but he guessed she could spot a lie in a split second.

While he drove to town he considered his options. Considering the iron weight that had settled in his belly, his options were few. If she wasn't pregnant, that was that. He could avoid her except for the times he bought cinnamon buns. Or he could date her, hoping to get lucky and take her to bed a whole lot more.

If she was pregnant, then that made things easier. Sort of. He would marry her and move her out to the ranch, where his future son would learn the cattle business. Or he could stop short of marrying her and instead get partial custody of the infant, which didn't seem like a real good solution. He didn't know anything about babies, didn't know what he'd do with an infant. Unless the thought of a grandchild would lure his mother home from California.

He could ignore the whole thing and say it wasn't his, a solution he thought Lisette might be partial to. She didn't seem too thrilled with continuing their relationship in any way. But she liked him a little—or else they wouldn't be in this mess in the first place. It wasn't a solution that sat well with him. If he had a kid he was damn well going to be its father. Even if it was a girl.

Cal parked behind the bakery and hurried up the stairs to the back door. He was ready to make the leap into marriage, if that's what he had to do. He would do what had to be done.

He was ready to meet his fate, but when he knocked no one was at home. Fate wasn't ready for him—at least not here—so Cal went back down the stairs and around the block until he stood in front of the bakery. He ignored the crowds of people in town for the final weekend of the festival, didn't feel the wind as it blew winter-cold air around his neck, certainly didn't notice when someone across the street called his name. All he saw through the sparkling window was a woman with long dark hair wiping the glass counters clean with graceful motions.

She looked up, as if she felt his gaze upon her, and she stopped cleaning. The inside of the bakery was still lit so he could see her clearly. He held up his hands as if to ask, "Well?"

Lisette hesitated, then nodded 'yes.' And that was when his heart stopped

9

"Not all of those who know their minds know their hearts as well."
—François, Duke de la Rochefoucauld (1613-1680)

"I DON'T NEED your help," Lisette said, wrestling with the cake boxes.

"Yeah, right," Cal said, lifting the heavy box out of her arms. "You can do this all by yourself."

"I can," she insisted, but Cal knew otherwise. These damn cakes were heavy and she still had to put the silly thing together after they got the pieces into the Wedding Bell Blues party room.

The little girls carried shopping bags full of decorations, Lisette carried two smaller boxes of cake and Cal followed them through the back door into the room that would hold a wedding reception in about two hours. He wasn't sure how he got into this, except that Lisette refused to discuss her pregnancy with him until she finished her work. And he was beginning to realize the woman was a fiend for work.

"So, is this where you want the reception?" The room was constructed of logs, with a couple of large picture windows on two of the walls. Heavy beams crossed the soaring ceiling and someone had twined little white lights around them, probably to give the place a festive look.

"What reception?" She set her boxes on a small corner table that was covered with a red-checked cloth.

"Ours."

She ignored him. "I hope this is where they wanted the cake. Mona took the directions, so I'm not—"

"Lisette," Cal said, lifting her fingers from the white boxes. Her hands were cold, so he held them between his to warm them. "Sweetheart, please talk to me."

"Please let me do my job," she countered, but she didn't pull her hands from his. He stood very close to her, his back to the rest of the room so they had a little privacy. The girls were unpacking the bags and chattering to themselves at a nearby table.

"In a minute," he promised, bringing her hands to his lips. He thought she jumped when his lips grazed her fingertips. Cal knew he had her complete attention now, which was exactly what he wanted. "You taste like frosting," he whispered.

"Butter cream," she murmured. "The bride wanted butter cream frosting on a vanilla cake with red roses."

"Nice," he said, moving his lips across her fingertips. "When are you going to marry me?"

"I can't—"

He didn't want to hear her refuse or argue, so he moved to cut off her words with his mouth. He still held her hands so she couldn't move away and he kissed her with the ferocity of a man who hadn't kissed his woman for months. Sweet, he thought, and hot. Very hot. It didn't take much for the two of them to ignite, a promising thought for the honeymoon. His tongue swept across her lips and they parted for him. Just like that, she was his. Warm, willing and passionate, she dissolved in his arms as if she wanted him as much as he'd thought about taking her. If they'd only been alone, was his thought before his brain shut down and his body wanted only one thing, to feel his woman's bare skin against his hands and tongue and—

"Mommy," a high-pitched voice interrupted. "Where do you want me to put the groom?"

He lifted his mouth slowly to whisper in Lisette's

ear. "In the bride's bed, of course. What do you say?"

"No bride, no groom, no bed."

Cal groaned and released her. "I can see you're going to be difficult about this."

"I have tiers to assemble."

He took one longing look at her mouth and thought of more interesting things to do than build cake. "All right," he said. "And what do you want me to do?"

She shrugged. "Watch the girls?"

"I can do that." He turned to see Cosette trying to balance the ceramic bride on her head while Amie's tiny fingers headed toward a container of frosting. "No problem," he said, sounding braver than he felt. "It'll be a piece of cake."

"YOU CAN CROSS the boy off your list," Mac declared in answer to Ella's question. "We've got a plan of our own."

"Really." Ella didn't like the sound of that. Whoever heard of a man knowing what was best? Except Father, of course, but the longer she thought about Father's decisions, the more she wondered if he had done what was best for his daughters or for himself. He'd certainly never thought any man was good enough for either one of his daughters, and up until now Ella had tended to believe that herself. "Tell me more," she said, holding the phone away from her ear a little more. Mac's voice tended to be rather loud.

"Well," Mac drawled, and she heard the satisfaction in his voice. "Cal is bound and determined to marry the woman, so that's what he's going to do."

"And when is the wedding?" Ella saw Louisa's head bob up from the newspaper at that question, so she shook her head to tell her sister that nothing was official.

"We're working on that part." Now Mac didn't sound so confident.

"Are they engaged, then, with a lovely diamond ring to show off?"

"Well, no, not yet."

"Has she accepted his proposal?" Ella sat down at the kitchen table and looked out the window as she waited for Mac to explain. Surely the man didn't think that he would succeed with this match without help. Her help.

"Darn, Ella, this is private information!"

"So was the pregnancy kit," she countered. "Where would you be without that information? And I assume somehow the child is his."

"Well, we wouldn't be goin' to all this trouble if it was someone else's!" Mac shouted, which caused

Ella to hold the phone farther away from her ear. She waited for a moment until she heard his breathing steady.

"So there is no engagement, meaning he has asked and she has refused."

"I guess you could put it like that. Calder usually gets what he wants, Ella, so I'm putting my money on him to win."

"That's a very nice gambling metaphor, Mac-Kenzie, but we're supposed to be discussing matrimony."

"We are?" Now he sounded amused.

"I am calling to find out if you need our help—my sister's and my help—to finalize the romance, if that's what it is. In other words, are we still involved or not?"

"Ella, you always did know too much for your own good, with a sharp tongue and—"

"Never mind my tongue," Ella snapped, causing Lou to drop her tea cup onto the table. The handle broke and Lou burst into tears. "The Hearts Club is ready to move on to another match, but we committed to Calder and we will put all of our energies into helping him if that's what is required."

"*Required?*" Mac repeated. "Not a damn thing's required. This festival's supposed to raise money for stuff for the town, not give you an excuse to stick your nose into people's business. Aren't you taking this matchmaking stuff a step too far?"

"What does that mean?" Ella didn't like anyone criticizing her matchmaking ideas. In fact, it made her want to bang the receiver on the counter a few times, but she reminded herself that she was a lady and resisted destroying the phone.

"You always were a mouthy woman, Ella. All prickly and stuck up, like there was no one good enough for you."

"That's not true." Odd how much those words hurt, even at age eighty-one. A woman had feelings, no matter how many wrinkles she wore or how much gray hair she looked at in the mirror. "You asked for my help, remember?"

"Yes, Ella, I do. And now I'm asking if you want to have supper together Sunday."

"What?" She felt as if she'd heard wrong. "What are you talking about?"

"Sunday supper," he repeated. "At the high school cafeteria. I think we should sit together and argue in person."

"How tempting."

"Five-thirty, then, unless you still think you're too good for a Brown," the old man had the nerve to say before he hung up on her.

"Ella?" Louisa held the dustpan with the broken cup pieces inside. "What was that all about?"

"Robert MacKenzie Brown always was an irritating man," Ella murmured, but she smiled as she hung up the phone.

"I FEEL LIKE a prize brood mare."

Cal glanced toward her and then back to the gravel road that led to the ranch. "Cheer up. You weigh less."

"This is a mistake, I just know it." She shouldn't have agreed to this. He'd been so helpful last night that she'd felt like she owed him a favor. He'd probably planned it that way.

"How can having dinner at the ranch be a mistake?"

"Your grandfather knows everything, doesn't he?"

"Like what?"

"Everything." She hoped he'd say no.

"Yes."

She groaned as quietly as she could so her daughters, strapped into seat belts in the back of Cal's SUV, couldn't hear. "What must he think?"

"He thinks we should get married, of course."

"Could we get through the evening without saying that word, please?"

"Married?" He slowed the car as they approached the cluster of buildings that comprised the house, barns and various garages and sheds. "I doubt it. Mac's pretty excited. He thinks you're going to bake your grandfather-in-law cinnamon rolls every morning."

"I can't marry you, I can't live out on the ranch and I can't give up my business."

"And I can't let my son grow up as a bastard."

"Shhh," she said. "The girls will hear you."

"It's what folks will call their brother—or sister. This is a small town," he said, echoing Maggie's words from yesterday. "People have opinions. People talk."

"Yes," she said, remembering the tabloid reporters hanging around her house. "It's like that in big cities, too."

"Then you see what has to be done." He parked the car and turned off the engine.

"Just because I understand what you're saying doesn't mean I'm rushing into marriage. Surely we can work something else out."

"There's only one solution, Lisette."

"You don't want to get married. What kind of life would this be for either one of us?" It was the wrong question to ask when she looked at the prosperous ranch spread out before her. The girls unhooked their seatbelts and scrambled out of the car when Cal opened the door. A large black dog bounded up to greet them, his tail wagging furiously. Mac opened the kitchen door and waved. It was a scene out of *Bonanza*, the perfect family coming home for Saturday supper.

She wished she didn't like him, but wishing didn't help at all, because she also wished she had never lost all sense and made love with a charming rancher eight days ago. Mac looked like he wanted to hug her as she approached the door, so she put a white bakery box in his arms.

"Chocolate cake," she told him.

"You're a fine woman," the old man declared. "And I'm glad to see you back here again."

"The scene of the crime," Cal whispered as they passed the kitchen table.

"How can you joke about it?" She turned to gaze up at him and then wished she hadn't. He was irresistible when he teased.

"That night has become one of my fondest memories. When we're married I'll send everyone to town so you and I can be alone in the kitchen again."

She blushed, much to her embarrassment, but from then on Cal was on his best behavior. "Mac, meet Cosette and Amie. Girls, this is Grandpa Mac."

Lisette turned to stare at him, but Cal ignored her. Mac didn't seem to mind the nickname.

"We're gonna go see those horses you're gonna ride," the old man said, ushering the girls toward the door. "And I'm the guy who's gonna teach you how."

Cosette's eyes grew wide. "Are you a cowboy?"

"Yes, darlin', one of the best." He winked at Lisette and then took her daughters outside. Cal shut the door behind him.

"Alone again," he said.

"I'd say you and your grandfather had this all planned."

"Did you think you're going to marry someone stupid?" He smiled down at her. "Come on. I'll show you the house."

Lisette took off her coat and handed it to him. "I'd like that." She'd like anything that kept them both on their feet. He put his hand on her back and guided her through the kitchen and down the hall.

"You've seen all this before," he said, as they entered the enormous living room. He ushered her past dark leather furniture and a stone fireplace toward another hall. "The bedrooms," he said, "are down here."

"I don't—" She was going to say that she didn't

need to see the private areas of the house, but Cal interrupted.

"You should see what you're getting into, where the girls will sleep and how this will work out." With that said, he showed her the first bedroom on the right. "Twin beds, if you want the girls to sleep together. Every room has its own bathroom, thanks to my mother. She had the place redone about twenty years ago."

Of course it was lovely, a guest room suited for either a man or a woman with its log walls, long windows that faced a pasture, bright quilts on the beds and braided rugs on the wood floor.

"Think they'll like it?" He draped his arm loosely over her shoulder.

"Anyone would."

"Good." He sounded relieved. "Come on, there's more."

And there was. A small unused study, a cluttered office, two more beautifully furnished guest rooms and finally, at the end of the wide hall, the master bedroom. Lisette stopped in the doorway.

"You'll be safe," he assured her, his calloused thumb caressing the nape of her neck before he released her. "For now. Go on in."

She'd expected to see a masculine room, and that is exactly how she would describe it. A huge four-poster bed made from peeled logs took up a large portion of the room, but Cal surprised her by pointing out a burgundy velvet and satin crazy quilt hung on the wall.

"It's been in the family for about a hundred and fifty years," he said. "But anything you don't like in here we can change."

"I'm not moving in," Lisette told him, but she couldn't help moving closer to the quilt to see the delicately embroidered birds and parasols. "Do you know who made it?"

"It came with one of the Brown brides many years ago. My mother thought about taking it with her when she moved, but decided it belonged on the ranch."

"Your mother hung it here?" She looked around the rest of large corner room. Long windows framed views of distant mountains, a burgundy rug covered most of the floor and framed photographs covered a large portion of the log walls.

"Eventually," he said. "Traditionally it's hung in the master bedroom to greet the new bride. That's you." Cal gently lifted her chin with his index finger. "I put it up this morning. To welcome you."

"That's nice, but—"

"Nice?" He lowered his head. "I'm not nice, sweetheart." His lips skimmed across her cheek, brushed her lips, tickled her ear. "You're in my bedroom and we're alone and what I'm thinking would make you blush again."

She could feel the heat in her face already. "We should—"

"Leave?" His hands settled on either side of her waist and prevented her from moving. "Nope."

"We should—" she tried again, knowing full well that she didn't want to step out of the embrace.

"Make love in the bed? Good idea, but it'll have to be fast." His mouth feathered hers in teasing motions.

"Stop," Lisette whispered.

"Stop talking or stop kissing?"

Good question, she thought, as her palms slid along his shirt and lifted to his shoulders. Her reaction to this man never failed to surprise her. Strictly physical, she knew, but somehow she found him hard to resist. He lifted her easily, swung her gently into his arms and carried her across the room to the bed.

"Cal—"

"What now?" He dropped her in the middle of the mattress and followed her down, his legs straddling hers.

"We can't do this," she managed to say, though she welcomed the heat from his body. She really should have more self-control, she reminded herself.

He lifted his head and frowned. "Because of the baby? Really?"

"No, not because of the—" She couldn't say it, because she wasn't ready to make it real. Despite the positive blood test and the aversion to coffee, she wanted to wait before thinking of this as a real, live baby and the effect it would have on her life.

"The baby," he said, his eyes dark as he gazed down at her. "*Our* baby."

"Because I have two little girls who could walk in the door any minute. Because I already made one mistake and I'm trying not to make another. And because—" She reached up and touched his cheek. "There isn't enough time."

"Ah." His lips almost lifted in a smile. "Finally, the truth."

"I try very hard to tell the truth."

He kissed the fingers that trailed over his lips. "Admit, then, that you'd like nothing better than to spend the rest of the evening in this bed."

"You tempt me," she said. "Which is the problem."

"It's a good start." He urged her thighs wider and settled himself against her. "So's this."

"Ummm." Distracted by the solid heat of him between her legs, Lisette closed her eyes and forgot for a moment that she was a woman with responsibilities.

Until she heard those responsibilities calling "Mommy!" from a distant room.

Cal swore under his breath, but he was laughing when he rolled off of her and climbed off the bed.

"Come on," he said, taking her hand to tug her to a sitting position. "From now on, we have to work on our timing."

Lisette smoothed her hair, still braided down her back, and adjusted her sweater over her slacks. "You are a dangerous man, Calder Brown."

He took her hand, but instead of leading her from the bedroom, he surprised her by bringing her fingers to his lips. "Dangerous? No. Determined? Yes."

"Is that a warning?"

"It means I'm planning a wedding. Soon. Before you start to look pregnant and folks start counting on their fingers. All you have to do is show up."

"This isn't the right way to start a marriage," she said, wishing he would listen to her, just once.

"There are worse reasons to get married," Cal replied, his gaze dropping to her abdomen. "I guess I'll just have to convince you to give me a chance." He released her hand and gestured toward the bedroom door. "After you, sweetheart," he drawled, allowing Lisette to exit gracefully.

This was not going to be easy, she realized as she found Mac and her girls building a fire in the living room fireplace. By refusing to marry this man, she was denying her children a father and grandfather and herself a solution to the aching loneliness she disliked so intensely.

But no one should get married because she was lonely. It didn't make sense to marry a man who was almost a stranger, a man whose attraction was sexual and whose past was littered with women and good times. Calder Brown might want to do the right thing and become a father and husband, but nothing was said of love—not that she'd believe him if he said the words—and even less was said of fidelity and expectations.

If she ever married again, she wanted to be loved and she wanted it to last forever. And Calder, the charming rancher with the killer smile who had just tossed Amie onto his shoulders, never said anything about forever.

10

*"Passion often turns the cleverest man into an id-
iot and the greatest blockhead into someone
clever."*
—François, Duke de la Rochefoucauld

"I HAVEN'T BEEN to one of these things since I was
eighteen," Cal grumbled, shoving his hands in the
pockets of his khaki slacks. They stood with their
backs to the wall and watched the crowd mingling
around the cafeteria. "And even then it wasn't too
much fun, except that I had a hot date with Mary
Lou Benning after she finished washing dishes."

"You haven't missed much," Gabe said. "Except
for some damn good desserts. This year Marryin'
Sam donated all the pies and I think your girlfriend
over there donated all of the fancy cookies."

"My girlfriend?" Cal knew exactly where Lisette
was. She'd been arranging desserts on a couple of
the long tables along one wall of the high school cafeteria, a job that had taken more time than he'd figured. He should have known she'd make it look like

some fancy Paris dessert buffet and that she wouldn't talk to him for more than two minutes at a time until it was done. To perfection. "I'm not sure that's what I'd call her."

"You haven't taken your eyes off the dessert table and I've heard that you've taken up coloring as a hobby." Gabe folded his arms across his chest. "It doesn't take a genius to figure out what's going on."

"She's a beautiful woman."

"And your eyes bulged out of your head the minute she came out of that cake," his friend reminded him. "If I didn't know better, I'd think that the Bliss sisters got to you after all."

"Me? No way." What had gotten to him was a broken condom and had nothing to do with Miss Ella or Miss Louisa, but Cal didn't tell Gabe that. No one ever needed to know exactly what went on between him and Lisette, or even why they were going to get married so fast. "Besides," he reminded Gabe, "if they find a wife for me, then you, old pal, are next on their list."

"And the festival ends tonight," he said. "I'm safe for another year."

"Safe? In this town? Nobody's safe, festival or no festival." He watched Lisette rearrange a second tier of desserts. She'd made something that looked like steps so the plates would be on different levels. It looked really nice, so nice that he thought he ought to go over and tell her so. Women sure liked to be complimented when they made pretty things.

"I'd better go round up the kids and make sure they've gotten something to eat," Gabe said. "You'd better watch out, Calder, or you'll be walking down the aisle yourself real soon."

"Yeah." She looked as beautiful as ever tonight, with a long straight black skirt and a short white sweater with some kind of fluffy silk scarf knotted at her throat. Her hair was tied in a loose knot at the back of her neck and he wondered what it would be like to have that long hair brushing his chest as Lisette moved on top of him.

"Invite me to the wedding," Gabe said, clapping him on the shoulder before he moved toward the crowd gathered around the spaghetti and meatballs table.

"Wedding?" He followed his friend across the room. "What do you know about a wedding?"

Gabe turned around and shook his head as if he couldn't believe what he was seeing. "Forget I said anything. Owen has been looking for you. He and Suzanne want to have us over for dinner. They want us to pick a night and bring dates."

"Yeah?" Lisette would like that. She'd get to see him as a guy with married friends and not just the kind of party animal that expected women to jump out of big wooden cakes. He would hold Owen's little niece and show that he could hold babies without dropping them. "Sounds good."

The other man chuckled. "I'll see you later. Go find your lady, Calder. You're starting to look pathetic, in love at last."

"I'm not in love," Cal protested, then lowered his voice so no one could overhear the conversation as he stepped closer to his best friend. "I'm just trying to get married, that's all."

"Outside," Gabe said, the smile having disappeared from his face. He jerked his thumb towards the door that led to the school corridor. "Now."

"This kind of talk needs beer," Cal grumbled. So much for keeping things to himself. At least when he told Gabe he was going to be a father, his friend would be able to give him some pointers. And maybe even come up with a way to make Lisette see sense.

Ten minutes later Cal knew he'd been wrong. Gabe couldn't get past the idea of Cal wanting to get married so fast and Owen, who was coming inside as they were on their way out, only clapped him on the shoulder and told him that marriage was a pretty damn good way of life.

"She keeps saying she won't marry me," Cal said,

which caused his friends to howl with laughter. He glared at Owen. "How'd you get married in a week, Chase?"

"Wasn't easy," he said. "I was supposed to meet her at the courthouse, but Darcy's school bus got hit by old man Cameron and then the Bliss ladies and their friends stopped Suzanne at the gas station and kept her from leaving, so—"

"Cripes, Owen," Cal interjected. "You don't make it sound easy."

Owen shrugged. "It wasn't too bad. The tough part is making the decision."

"Sounds like the tough part for Cal here is convincing the lady he'd make a good husband." Gabe shook his head. "So it looks like you've got your work cut out for you, Calder."

"You'd be a father, too, to those little girls of hers," Owen pointed out. "You ready to do that?"

"They're nice kids." He didn't add that "Grandpa Mac" was going to give them riding lessons or that Cosette's tears when she had to say goodbye to "her" horse yesterday had made him feel like moving the whole family to the ranch right then and there, just to make the pretty little girl smile again.

"Something odd is going on," Gabe said, "but it's your business, Cal. I just hope you know what you're doing." He turned to Owen. "I'm going to go get some dinner. Are either one of you joining me?"

"I'll go find Suzanne," Owen said. "She got here early to help Darcy and the basketball teams cook spaghetti and now she's running around with her camera taking pictures for the paper. But maybe she'll have time to eat with us now."

"And I'll make Lisette stop fussing with the pies."

"I'll check on my kids and get us a table," Gabe said. "I saw Mac sitting with the Bliss ladies. Is he looking to get married again?"

"I doubt it," Cal said, as the men headed back inside the cafeteria. "He's more interested in my settling down than anything else."

"Looks like things are going to change at your place," Owen drawled. "Who's going to give Cal a bachelor party?"

Gabe laughed. "The big question is who's going to jump out of the cake?"

LISETTE MET Suzanne Chase at the dessert table. The slim redhead carried a fat toddler on her hip, a camera around her neck and looked at the arrangements of desserts as if she'd discovered heaven.

"I fell in love with this town the minute I tasted the apple pie," she confided, which made Lisette smile.

"You're the reporter, aren't you? I think you came to my coffee shop a couple of weeks ago." She held out her hand. "I'm Lisette Hart."

"Suzanne Chase," she said, shaking her hand. "I'm also in love with your apple tarts."

"I'm glad to hear it." So this was the woman who met Owen Chase, the recipient of the bachelor party, and married him a week later. "Next time you stop in, knock on the kitchen door and say hello."

"I'd like that," Suzanne said, gently removing the leather camera strap from the baby's fist. "I haven't met too many women my age yet." She laughed when the toddler protested. "This is Mel, my husband's niece. She's starting to get a mind of her own."

"It's a cute age," Lisette said, allowing herself to think of her pregnancy for a second. If it was a girl she would name her after her mother. If it was a girl maybe Calder would leave them all alone. Odd that it wasn't a very happy thought.

"Would you mind holding her for a minute? I'd love to get a picture of this table for the paper. They're letting me freelance a little."

"Of course I wouldn't mind." She moved away from the table and held out her arms. The baby didn't mind going to her, but she did keep her eyes on her new mother while Suzanne photographed the desserts from various angles.

Lisette didn't know that Cal was nearby until she heard someone say his name. She turned to see the rancher staring at her as his grandfather, seated at a nearby table, called him. Calder smiled and kept heading her way and Lisette found herself smiling back. She knew he would have something entertaining to say, something that would make her laugh.

"Sweetheart," he said, in that familiar drawl that made her very aware that she was a woman with intimate knowledge of this particular man. "I heard you've been looking for me, so here I am."

He knew she hadn't from the way his eyes twinkled.

"I don't look for trouble," she said, but she couldn't help smiling. The baby shrieked and stretched toward him, so Cal lifted the child from Lisette's arms.

"At least someone's glad to see me," he said to the baby who reached for the brim of his hat.

"She knows you?"

"I get around," he said, winking at her at the same time he kept the little girl from flinging his hat to the floor. "I came to get you for dinner."

"Oh, good," Suzanne said, putting her camera back in its case, "you're eating with us."

"Well—"

"Come on," Cal said, putting his arm around Lisette's shoulders as if they were a couple. "You've met Gabe and Owen and you know Suzanne, so you can't escape. You know I get depressed when you're not around."

Suzanne laughed. "I heard he was a flirt, Lisette. You'd better watch out."

"Too late," Cal said. "She's stuck with me, at least for tonight."

Yes, Lisette thought, wishing she didn't enjoy the warmth of his arm against her back. She was stuck with him, all right, for as long as he was interested in becoming a father. She didn't know what would happen after that, but she needed to guard her heart against the man. He was entirely too charming, too handsome and too likable.

And he looked too damn good carrying that baby.

"Put me down."

Cal ignored the command and kept a firm grip on her. "I'm taking you to the truck," he said, "so quit arguing about it."

Lisette wanted to protest again, but decided that she would close her eyes so she couldn't see the curious looks of the people at the spaghetti supper. She was cradled in Cal's arms and truthfully was relieved not to be walking. "I just got dizzy for a few seconds," she said to his chest.

"Yeah. I guessed that when you turned white and grabbed the edge of the table."

"My coat—"

"Suzanne's following us with your stuff."

She heard him push the door open and felt the cold air hit her face. Lisette opened her eyes and took a deep breath, but the dizziness returned with a vengeance. "This is embarrassing."

"Yeah," Cal said. "Miss Ella was glaring at me like I was kidnapping you. She probably thinks I'm carrying you off to bed."

"Let's not talk about that." Sex had gotten her in this predicament in the first place.

"I *am* carrying you off to bed," Cal said, sounding very pleased with himself. "When we get there sex is optional."

"How thoughtful of you."

"But just so you know, if you want me," he said, standing her on her feet but keeping a firm hand around her waist, "you don't have to beg."

"Thank you for being so considerate, Cal."

"That's the kind of guy I am," he said, giving her a quick smile. He opened the truck's passenger door and lifted her onto the seat. "There you go, sweetheart. Can you sit up okay for a few minutes 'til we get to your place?"

"I think I'll be fine." Lisette took another deep breath of cold air and felt her head clear. "It was the coffee smell," she explained. "It got the best of me this time."

"When do you see Doc Hawley?"

"Next week."

Suzanne ran up and delivered Lisette's jacket and purse. "Was there anything else?"

"No, but thank you. I'm not sure what happened in there, except that the room started to spin."

"Go home and get some rest," the redhead said.

"I will," she promised. Cal was in the truck and ready to start the engine after Suzanne closed the passenger door. "I'm feeling better," she assured him, as he backed up the truck and turned toward the street.

"Good." But the look he gave her was anything but convinced that she was fine.

She didn't remember feeling this sick this early in her pregnancy. Even if she'd always known almost immediately of the changes pregnancy brought to her body, this time felt different. Maybe it was stress—the kind that came from single motherhood and the divorce and the move to a new town and starting her own business.

"Is there anyone I can call?"

Lisette turned towards him. "Call?"

"Parents? Sisters? Relatives who could help you out for a while?"

"I'm an only child. My parents died when I was five," she explained. "My grandmother and I left France after that and moved to Los Angeles, where Mamere had friends. She died seven years ago, right after my marriage." There was no one else, except some distant cousins in France she heard from at Christmastime. She leaned her head back against the headrest and thought about all the orders she had taken for Thanksgiving desserts. "I'll see if Mona can work more hours."

"Why don't you move out to the ranch for a while? Mac can help with the girls and you can get some rest."

"I can't."

"Because of the business?"

"That's one of the reasons," she said. He was silent until they reached the parking area behind her apartment.

"Don't move," he said, shutting off the engine. He came around to the passenger door, which she had already opened, and took her in his arms.

"I can walk."

He reluctantly set her on her feet. "Hold onto me, just in case you get dizzy again."

"I'm better," she assured him, taking another breath of clean Montana air. "It was awfully hot in there, don't you think?"

"Sure." He kept his arm around her until they were at her kitchen door and she unlocked it. Cal followed her inside and looked around, as if he was surprised by the emptiness. "Where are the girls?"

"At a friend's house," she said.

"Whose?"

"Maggie Moore's."

"Maggie has them? I wondered why she wasn't at the high school tonight."

Lisette laid her coat and purse over a kitchen chair. "It's her daughter's birthday, so she invited both Cosette and Amie to the party."

"Shouldn't you be lying down or something?" He stood there, taking up a lot of space in the small kitchen, his hands on his hips as he tried to figure out how to help.

"In a while." Lisette wanted to crawl into bed and burrow under the covers, but she didn't want to say that to Calder. He would most likely follow her into her bedroom to make sure she was okay and one thing would lead to another and they'd have their clothes off. "You don't have to worry."

"You're going to have a baby," he said. "Of course I worry."

She turned and walked into the living room, switched on a lamp next to the couch and sat down. She untied her black boots and kicked them aside. "There. Now I'm feeling better."

He hesitated in the doorway. "Don't you think you should be in bed?"

"Not yet." She wiggled her toes and leaned back against the cushions. "You don't have to stay. Go back to the party. Maybe you'll win something at the raffle."

"There's nothing I need," the man said, crossing the room. He drew up a stool and sat down in front of her, then took her stockinged feet in between his hands. "Can you let me act like a future father for a few minutes?"

"And what do you think a future father does exactly nine months before the baby is born?" She closed her eyes as he caressed her feet, massaging the sore spots with just the right pressure.

"He takes care of his woman."

"Ummmmm," she murmured. "You're good at this."

"Thanks."

"And I'm not your woman." Although another few minutes of this and she would be, Lisette decided. The man had the golden touch when it came to rubbing away aches and pains.

"Sure you are. We're getting married, remember?" His voice was soft and his hands continued to work their magic.

"Marriage is not a good idea. Take my word for it."

"You need me," he reminded her. "For when you get dizzy and for when your feet hurt."

"Or I could buy smelling salts and soak my feet in a bucket of hot water."

"And here I thought Frenchwomen were romantic." He gave her big toes a gentle tug.

"I used to be," she admitted, feeling Calder's fingers circle her ankles. "And then I got divorced."

"Tell me." His large hands caressed her calves, then back down to her feet once again.

"Tell you what?" Her bones were turning to mush and so was her determination to keep Calder out of her bed.

"What did he do to hurt you?" The massage continued.

She sighed from sheer contentment. "I don't want to talk about it."

"Just tell me if he could be a problem."

"He won't." Not from prison, thank goodness. She kept her eyes closed and the dizziness stayed away, the massage continued and her bones turned to the consistency of heavy cream, until Cal removed his hands from her legs.

"Okay, sweetheart," he said. "Time for bed."

Lisette opened her eyes and couldn't help smiling up at him. Cal didn't return the smile.

"I'm carrying you," he said. "No arguments."

"Okay." He bent down and scooped her into his arms.

"Still dizzy?"

"No."

"Is it always this way?" He carried her around the corner and toward the bedrooms. The apartment was small, with the two bedrooms divided by a bathroom, a small hall separating them from the living room and kitchen.

"Being sick?" she asked. "No. I don't remember being dizzy like this before, with the girls. Though I could feel the changes right away and couldn't drink coffee."

"You work too hard." He set her on top of her double bed, her head on the pile of linen-covered pillows. "When do you have to pick up the girls?"

"I don't," she said, wishing he was in the bed with her. She'd like nothing more than to snuggle beside all that warmth and not feel so alone.

"They're spending the night. Amie was ecstatic at being a big girl."

"I don't want to leave you alone," he said, a worried look on his face. He sat down gingerly on the edge of the bed, making the mattress tip toward him. "What if something happens?"

"Like what?"

He shrugged. "I don't know. This whole pregnancy thing scares the living daylights out of me."

"You can walk away," Lisette offered, though she wondered how his absence would affect her. She liked him, liked being with him, had enjoyed making love to him that one incredible time. He made her laugh and he rubbed her toes and he bought coloring books.

"You don't know me very well." He reached out and caressed her cheek.

"Wild bachelor? Freedom-loving rancher? A man who takes trips to Las Vegas and has money to burn?"

"That was before," Cal said. "I'm afraid for you, not for myself."

"This could be a long nine months."

"Not if you marry me."

She covered his hand with her own, ran her fingertips over his knuckles. "How does that change things, Cal?"

"It gives me the right to take care of you. And it gives me the right to be a father to my child."

"It's too soon," Lisette insisted. "We're going much too fast."

"Not in Bliss, sweetheart," the man said, leaning forward to kiss her. "In this town folks make up their minds pretty damn quick and most of 'em *stay* married. Like it or not, the odds are with us."

"I wish I could believe that," she whispered, right before he kissed her.

11

"The strength of any plan depends on timing."
—*Montaigne (1533-1592)*

AND KISSING HER was Cal's downfall. Though he'd promised himself that he would not touch her, touching her was a temptation he couldn't resist. The woman lay on her bed and looked at him with those dark green eyes that made a man forget all the promises he made to himself. A gentleman wouldn't seduce a pregnant woman—a *dizzy* pregnant woman—or even attempt to kiss her.

But Calder Brown was no gentleman. At least not where Lisette Hart was concerned. His mouth found hers, his chest brushed her breasts, his hands tangled in her hair on either side of the pillow. He felt her hands curl around the back of his neck and took that as a sign that the lady didn't mind being kissed. He wondered if she'd mind more than kissing, if dizzy pregnant women wanted to have sex with the men who were the reason for being dizzy and pregnant in the first place.

So he asked, when he lifted his mouth from hers and caught his breath. "Are you going to send me back to the ranch?"

"I think you'd better stay here," Lisette said, the barest of smiles showing that she wasn't upset at the question, didn't think he was a horny beast out for what he could get. "In case I need you."

"Well," he drawled, taking a strand of her hair and feeling its softness between his fingers. "You may be surprised how much you like having me around."

"Cal?"

"What?"

"I do like having you around," she admitted, dropping her hands to his shirtfront where she began to unfasten the buttons.

"A compliment at last."

"And I don't want to be alone tonight," she confessed.

"And I've never made love to a pregnant woman before." This could be his first—and his last—time, depending on Lisette's plans for their future. He didn't know how to tell her that this was special for him, that she was someone unique, that discovering he was going to be a father had been like Christmas morning and the Fourth of July all rolled into one. "Are there any special instructions?"

"As long as you don't dangle me upside down over the side of the bed we should do just fine." She laughed at the expression on his face, which made him swoop down and kiss her until she stopped. And then there was no more laughter, only heat and longing and a frenzied attempt to remove each other's clothes without breaking the kiss for more than seconds at a time. The last to hit the floor were Lisette's black silk panties, reminding Cal of the outfit she'd worn for the party.

"You should always wear black lace," he murmured, skimming his lips across her flat abdomen.

"I do."

"See? We're getting to know each other better." He kissed a spot beneath her navel. "It's hard to believe there's anyone in there."

"You'll believe it in a few months," she whispered. "When I'm waddling."

"I won't mind," he said, his mouth moving lower. "You'll be a beautiful waddler."

"Cal—"

"Shhh," he murmured. "I'm getting to the good part."

Her laughter stopped when he touched her. She was slick and wet and opened easily when he ran his fingers and then his tongue along her cleft. Sweet and hot under his mouth, tempting him as her thighs fell apart and she made a sound of surprise. He wanted to please her, needed to touch and taste and discover what gave this woman—*his* woman—pleasure.

Cal wanted to please her. And he intended to make her his.

Just in case there was any doubt.

WHILE SHE LAY sleeping, Calder realized that his future wife was a passionate woman. Oh, he'd had the incredible memory of kitchen sex with Lisette. He'd never been more surprised in his life, but stranger things had happened and there'd been some times in his truck with other women that had certainly been exciting and made him glad he was young, healthy and alive.

But making love to Lisette had damn near knocked him out. Now he lay here in bed, tucked under flowered sheets and fluffy blankets, stark naked and hoping she'd wake up so he could make love to her again. Although attempting to do it in the next half hour would probably embarrass him, he knew he'd die trying. A man had his pride.

So she was tucked against his body, all satin skin and long hair, while she slept. The apartment was dark and quiet without the children, but so small Cal had bumped his head on a bathroom ceiling beam. He would move them to the ranch as soon as possible after the wedding. He could find someone to run the bakery, to bake pies and cream puffs and cinnamon rolls, so that Lisette could get some rest. He gathered her closer against him and wondered at the change in his life in just a few days.

Now he had a wedding to plan. Somehow he didn't think Lisette would want to elope to Las Vegas. Maybe a party at the ranch, something for a couple hundred of his closest friends. It was not every day a man became a husband and a father at the same time.

"HE DUMPED ME, just walked away with someone else, right in front of everyone," Mona said, wiping away her tears with a paper towel. "Now what am I going to do?"

Lisette didn't have the faintest idea, but she couldn't send Mona to wait on customers until the girl had stopped crying. Hopefully no one would show up before six, even though it was Monday. "Have a cup of tea," she said, "and tell yourself you were too good for him."

"He said he was bored. *Bored*," she repeated, sniffling. "And here I thought we were going to get engaged during the festival."

"Honey, the festival's over," Lisette said as gently

as she could. The timer buzzed, so she hurried across the room to take the apple tarts out of the oven. "Someone else will come along, someone much better."

"You think?" Mona hiccupped. "Really?"

"I certainly do."

"Absolutely," a male voice declared. "Either one of those Lackland boys is nothing but trouble, Mona. Not worth the powder to blow them up."

They both turned to see Cal standing at the foot of the stairs.

"What are you—oops," Mona said, looking at her boss and then back to Calder. "Never mind."

"Good morning." Lisette decided to pretend that the man came down her stairs every morning, although Mona's mouth still hung open. The truth was, Lisette was ridiculously happy to see him, which didn't make any sense at all. She should have hoped he would leave quietly, by the back door. Instead, larger than life, his dark hair still damp from a shower, he was in her bakery kitchen and looking for all the world as if he stood there every morning.

"Good morning." He strolled over and smelled the apple tarts. "Are those for breakfast?"

She heard herself say, "Sit down and I'll fix you a plate. There's coffee out in front. You can help yourself."

"I'll get it." Mona jumped up and headed for the swinging door. "I could use a cup myself."

Lisette waited for the girl to leave before she spoke. "I didn't think you'd be up so early."

"I'm a rancher," he reminded her. "It goes with the job." He looked as if he wanted to kiss her, so Lisette turned around and fussed with the tarts, making sure she picked out the biggest one for Cal. "I've been thinking about the wedding," he said. "How about something at the ranch?"

Lisette took a ceramic plate from the stack by the sink and fixed the tart on it, along with a dessert fork.

"I didn't think you'd want to go to Vegas," he continued. "But if there's some place else you have in mind, let's get it done."

Mona returned with the coffee, but kept it carefully away from Lisette. She set it down on the table and, after a quick look at Cal, went back to the front room without saying a word.

"So?" Calder asked. "When and where?"

"I can't talk about this now," Lisette said. "I'll burn something."

Cal looked surprised, but he went over to the table and retrieved his coffee. "Is it okay if I drink it in this room?"

"Just don't wave it around in front of me, all right?"

He took a couple of gulps and then smiled at her. "How'd you sleep?"

"Someone woke me up once or twice."

"He isn't sorry."

"Neither am I." Another timer went off, so Lisette busied herself with the rolls in the lower oven until they were safely on a cooling rack.

"What time do you get done?"

"I close at four, but—"

"I'll pick you up. We'll have dinner at the ranch."

"Cal—"

He set down his cup. "What's wrong?"

Everything, Lisette wanted to say, as she stood in her kitchen looking at the rancher she'd spent the night in bed with. He looked sleepy and yet restless, all male as he discussed a wedding the way he might discuss having a barbeque.

"Lisette?" Cal walked over and put his hands on her shoulders.

"Don't you have cows to milk or rope or brand?"

"You're trying to get rid of me," he said, looking amused. "You women are all alike. You use us men for our bodies and then won't have anything to do with us the morning after." He kissed her briefly, then tugged the braid of hair that fell over her shoulder. "I know when I'm not wanted, sweetheart, so I'll head home and get to work."

"That's a good idea." And would give her time to bake and think, to have a cup of peppermint tea and go over the orders for Thanksgiving, only a few days away.

"When are the girls coming back?"

"Around eight. Maggie's dropping the girls off at school and then bringing Amie here."

"I'll pick you up at five," Calder said.

She shook her head. "No. We've got to slow down."

His eyebrows rose. "Isn't it a little late for that?"

"Go away, Cal," Lisette ordered. "I've got work to do." She turned around and opened the oven door to check on the breads so she wouldn't have to see him leave or counter another suggestion to be together. She was in deep, deep trouble, because Lisette knew she'd gone and done the unthinkable.

She'd fallen in love with Calder Brown.

And the only thing she could do now was hope he'd never notice.

"I DO NOT UNDERSTAND why you are behaving this way." Ella's cup clattered in its saucer as she set it down.

"We're talking about Thanksgiving, Ella," her sister explained. "Cameron has invited us to his granddaughter's house for dinner. I think it sounds lovely."

"Not if Cam's daughter's girl is as big an idiot as Cam is," Ella grumped. "I can't imagine what that turkey will taste like."

"Ella! That's not nice," her sister said, but she was more occupied in heating a cinnamon bun in the microwave than she was discussing their dinner plans. "Besides, I think Cam said they were buying a turkey all cooked and stuffed, because Becky—that's the granddaughter—had twins a few months ago."

"Twins," Ella repeated, hoping her sister would hear the horror in her voice. "Thanksgiving with infant twins is your idea of a lovely holiday?"

"Cam and I want to spend it together," she said, having decided her breakfast had spent enough time in the microwave. She brought her plate to the table and sat down. "What else would we do?"

"We have options," Ella reminded her. "As always."

"I refuse to go to the mayor's house again," Lou declared. "Those martinis he served the last time gave me a headache for three days. And I am not going to cook a monstrous turkey for the two of us. Last year we ended up throwing most of it away, even though Pete and his sister came over." She took a bite of her cinnamon roll and then licked her fingers. "I'd like to see those twin babies, Ella. Cam said they're almost over that colicky stage."

Ella decided it was time to put her foot down before she was trapped in a dining room full of Camerons and screaming babies on Thursday. "While I hate to interfere with your quest for a love life, Lou, I can't imagine a mother of twins is going to look forward to entertaining two more guests at Thanksgiving."

"Well," Lou said, a concerned look on her round face, "I suppose it might be an imposition, though Cam said she was looking forward to meeting us. Where else would we go?"

"Funny you should ask," Ella said, leaning forward. "You have frosting on your chin, Lou." She waited for Louisa to wipe it off with her linen napkin. Ella didn't believe in using too many paper products. "Robert—Mac—has invited us to his ranch."

"He has? Why?"

"He hinted that Mrs. Hart would be there and an announcement might be made."

"A *wedding* announcement?"

"Of course. He thought we might like to be there, since we were part of the matchmaking effort."

Louisa smiled knowingly. "And you, of course, wouldn't mind seeing Mac again, would you?"

"What is that supposed to mean?"

"You liked him once," her sister said, forking another piece of her breakfast bun. "You liked him very much. And now you like him again."

"What I'd *like*," Ella said, wishing her sister would refrain from getting personal, "is to see the happy ending of our matchmaking on Calder's behalf."

"Well, I suppose that would be nice," Louisa conceded. "And Lisette will bring dessert, I'm sure, which would be a treat. And her daughters are very sweet-looking."

"And well-behaved," Ella pointed out. "Not like most of the children we see these days."

"Well, all right," Lou said. "I'll break the news to Cam that we can't spend Thanksgiving together."

"I'm sure he'll manage to contain his disappointment."

"Don't be mean, Ella." Louisa ate the last bit of cinnamon bun. "Cam is smarter than he looks."

"Which might possibly be said for most men," Ella said. "Though of course there are no guarantees."

"NO TIME," Lisette declared once again, when Cal arrived in the bakery. She watched as Amie hurried over to give him a hug, but Lisette resisted doing the same thing. Saying she was busy wasn't a lie; the truth kept Calder at arm's length, which was exactly where Lisette wanted him. Hot sex, night-long passion and whispered intimacies wouldn't make any of this any better.

She was in love with him and she was probably going insane at the same time. Maybe it was the town's fault after all, or something in the water. Matchmakers and weddings and tourists looking for love combined to give Bliss an eerie matrimonial madness.

And, like it or not, she was in the middle of it, because Amie was now perched on Cal's shoulders and smiling as if she'd won a new box of markers.

"We're going shopping," Cal said, reaching for Amie's coat. He handed it up to her while the child giggled. "We have a dinner date tomorrow, remember?"

"Yes."

"How are you feeling?"

"Never better," she fibbed, knowing if she told him that her dizziness and nausea continued that he would never leave her to do her work.

"Then give me a kiss and send us on our way," he said, bending down enough to make Amie squeal.

His kiss was brief, but the heat in his gaze made Lisette blush. "I've missed you," was all he said, and Lisette knew exactly what he meant. She'd missed him, too.

"Get out of here," she told him, unable to resist his smile. "I have work to do." Mona rallied from her broken heart long enough to learn how to make pies, though Lisette wouldn't trust the pie crust dough to anyone but herself.

"Tomorrow you rest," Cal said. "And we're going to make some plans." With that statement, he turned around and headed toward the door. Amie didn't even look back and wave, but Mona closed the cash register and sighed.

"He's gorgeous, Mrs. Hart."

"Yes."

"You're so lucky."

"Yes." And she knew it. How many other men would insist on marrying a strange woman they'd impregnated by accident? How many men would bring coloring books to her daughters and worry about her health and rub her feet and make love to her with such knowing passion?

But with fatherhood came responsibilities which Calder couldn't even imagine at present, in his "I'm going to be a father" golden haze. And they had not talked of love—which would be silly—and commitment, which wouldn't. Or divorce and child custody, which was inevitable when one started a marriage with such an odd set of circumstances.

It all boiled down to one thing, Lisette knew, retreating to her kitchen and the ticking timer on the counter. She would love and adore the man and, as soon as the thrill of marriage wore off, he would be gone—to other women and other adventures.

And having said "I do" in front of a minister wouldn't stop the pain.

"YOU'RE JOKING, RIGHT?"

"Nope." Mac carried seven dinner plates to the long kitchen table and started setting them out. "I'll sit at the head of the table and you can sit at the foot. The ladies will sit on one side and your little family on the other."

"You invited them *here? Today?*"

"I sure did. Kinda thought they might be lonely, with no family and all."

"They don't strike me as lonely old ladies, Mac. In fact, they scare me to death."

"Get over it." He eyed the arrangements and frowned. "Do you think we need some more decorations?"

"You already bought out the Hallmark store," Cal pointed out. The table was covered with a bright orange cloth, the creases still there to show it was fresh out of the package. Each place setting had a turkey print paper napkin and a matching ceramic napkin holder. A bunch of ceramic autumn leaf candle holders were lined up in a neat row in the middle of the table and held golden candles, not yet lit.

"I think it looks right festive," Mac declared. "No one would know we haven't done this in a while."

"We haven't," Cal grumbled, but he had to admire the old man for making such a production out of it. "We watched football and ate tacos last year because Mom went to Mexico on some tour."

"There's no harm in turning on the TV before dinner, but we'll have to mind our manners when the ladies come."

"We'll serve drinks in the living room and mute the sound. That way we can see if Seattle ever has a chance against—what's wrong?"

"I forgot to get them little name tags."

"We all know who each other is." And they all certainly knew the Bliss sisters...and their reputations.

"No," Mac grumbled. "The ones for the table, telling folks where to sit."

"I'll tell them," Cal said. "I'm putting Lisette as close to me as I can get her."

"Just set a date for the wedding, will you? I'm

starting to get excited about this. And you'd better tell your mother soon, too, or we'll never hear the end of it."

"I'll call her tonight," Cal promised, knowing his mother would be on the next plane home as soon as she heard she was going to be a grandmother.

"We've never had a baker in the family before, though your grandmother knew her way around a kitchen. That woman could make biscuits that could make you cry."

"They should be here any minute." He'd bought games for the girls and more crayons and paper, just in case Amie was feeling artistic. Cosette's favorite pony was corralled nearby, so he'd be available for petting. And he had a nice little memento from Bozeman tucked in his shirt pocket, waiting for the right time to show Lisette. Calder walked over to the windows that fronted the drive. "What about your guests?"

"They're driving themselves," he said, "even though I offered to go to town and pick them up."

"Lord help us," Cal muttered. "Miss Louisa is a menace in that old car. Uh-oh." He spotted a gold sedan going faster than it should. "I think they're on their way now."

"Be nice," Mac said. "I never told you I was sweet on Ella once. If her father hadn't been against my showing up to court her, she might've been your grandmother."

"I wish you hadn't told me that."

"Well, son," his grandfather chuckled, stepping over to look out the window. "We've all got our dirty little secrets."

"I guess," Cal said, feeling the ring in his pocket. He would give her the ring, set the date and announce the wedding. And that would be that. Funny how scared he was that she'd say no.

12

"The heart has reasons which reason knows not of."
—Blaise Pascal (1623-1662)

"HE SEEMS VERY MUCH in love with you, dear." Miss Louisa beamed her approval from across the dining room table when, after dinner, their hosts were busy on the other side of the kitchen. "How lovely for you both."

"Thank you." Lisette didn't know what else to say, because she certainly couldn't tell Miss Louisa that the man was only doing his duty, because he wanted his child. And yet, Calder Brown had greeted her as if seeing her on his doorstep was the highlight of his Thanksgiving. Mac had given her a hug as if he hadn't seen her in months and then fixed her a cup of tea, making sure she was settled in the living room in the most comfortable chair until dinner was ready.

Miss Ella's expression was not so easy to read. The elderly woman appeared to approve of the children, the Thanksgiving dinner and the company, but she preferred to talk to the senior Mr. Brown instead of Calder. Their stories of growing up in Bliss had entertained everyone throughout dinner, even the children. And there had been moments when Lisette's gaze had locked with Calder's and she forgot to breathe.

"Excuse me for a moment," Lisette said to the ladies. "I'm going to go check on the girls." She found them in the living room, playing one of the games Cal provided. The television was showing the inevitable football game, but neither child noticed.

"Mommy?" Cosette raised her arms for a hug, so Lisette bent down and hugged both girls.

"Are you having fun?"

"I love it here," Amie declared. "Grandpa Mac said I can visit any time I want."

"Me, too," Cosette added. "And my pony remembered me. He smelled my hand and knew who I was. Cal said."

"Well, if Cal said—" Then it must be true.

Cosette nodded. "He asked me if I liked it here."

"And what did you say?"

Her daughter looked at her as if she'd lost her mind. "I said, 'I like it very much, Mr. Brown.' Was that okay?"

"Of course."

"I can get a pony, too," Amie insisted. "A little one that doesn't kick and likes little girls."

"Cal said?"

"Uh-huh." The child nodded, her interest returning to the game as her sister spun a cardboard wheel covered in numbers. Lisette reminded them of the bathroom's location and told them to come get her if they got lost. Neither child paid much attention to her, except Amie waved when she left.

"Hey." Calder met her in the hall. "I wondered where you went to."

"I checked on the girls."

"Are they okay?"

"Just fine. They're playing games and talking about ponies." She didn't protest when he took her hand and led her down the hall to his office.

"Don't mind the mess," he said, kicking the door shut behind them and turning the knob to lock it.

"What are you doing?" She knew the answer, because he gave her that charming sexy smile and tugged her into his arms.

"Playing games," he said, kissing her ear. "Talking about ponies. Do you ride?"

"No." She looped her arms around his neck while his lips trailed along her jaw and sent shivers down her skin.

"Drive a truck?" His hands slipped under her sweater and caressed the bare skin of her back. He

was hard against her hip and she wondered, for one
brief crazy second, if it was possible to make love on
the top of his cluttered desk.

"No."

"Play poker? Drink beer? Line dance?" He unhooked her bra and slid his right hand to cup her
breast.

"No, no and no. We have nothing in common,"
she whispered, dropping her hand to skim along
the hard length of him. "You should understand
that."

Cal groaned. "You'll marry me anyway, won't
you?"

Lisette forgot about everything in her life that
made sense and, with a little moan, answered,
"Yes."

And learned it was possible to consummate an
engagement on Cal's desk after all.

Her skirt slid up, his zipper slid down, and he
lifted her onto the desk and followed her down onto
the stacks of papers. Neither noticed when the papers slid to the floor or the pen holder tipped over
and an empty coffee cup fell into the wastebasket.
What mattered was having him inside of her, despite clothing and lace underwear and the distant
sounds of football on television. He put his hand on
her mouth when he entered her, a reminder to be
quiet when it felt so good she wished she could tell

him. When he'd filled her completely, he caressed her cheek and leaned to whisper in her ear as he made love to her until she came, quick and hard and trying not to make a sound. And then he joined her, as her tremors pushed him into an urgent release of his own.

"We're insane," Lisette whispered, even then wishing he didn't have to withdraw from her body so soon, and yet there was dessert to serve and children to care for and people who would expect intelligent conversation.

"Not insane," Cal said, lifting himself above her to fumble with his shirt pocket. A platinum band of diamonds and emeralds fell out onto her sweater. "Engaged."

"I TELL YOU, it was a sight to behold," Ella crowed to her friends while her sister demolished a stack of blueberry pancakes.

"The emerald and diamond ring?" Missy asked. "I'll bet it was."

"No, not the ring. Calder's face." Ella raised her voice, so she could be heard over the sounds of bowling. The Hearts Club had agreed to meet a little later today, due to Grace's family commitments, but having breakfast at ten on Saturday instead of eight was certainly noisier. "He was beaming upon our Mrs. Hart and she was smiling, too."

"True love," Louisa added. "That's what it looked like to me, despite everything."

They all knew that "everything" meant Lisette's pregnancy and the obvious reason for the match.

"But still," Ella mused, taking another sip of coffee. "They do make a lovely couple."

Grace agreed. "I hope she'll keep the bakery."

"And Ella got us invited to the wedding," Louisa announced. "We feel so lucky."

"My goodness," Missy breathed. "When *is* the wedding?"

"They agreed on two weeks from today, before Christmas, at St. Peter's. Cal's mother will want to be here for the ceremony, of course. And Mrs. Hart wanted time to train some staff to help her with the holiday orders."

Louisa added, "The little girls seemed happy about it. They're very sweet girls."

"Polite, too."

"Mrs. Hart must be a wonderful mother," Missy said with an envious sigh.

"Well," Ella declared. "That's the whole point, isn't it? Calder Brown wants to be a father."

"I THINK I'M going to be sick."

"No, you're not." Mac adjusted his grandson's collar and studied his tie. "You'll do. Just take deep breaths. Every man has second thoughts, you know, *nerves*, on his wedding day."

"Don't say 'wedding day,'" Calder begged. "I shouldn't have had that big breakfast."

"Too bad your mother insisted on cooking," the old man said with a sigh. "She never really had a knack with eggs and bacon."

"I should have stuck with the cinnamon rolls brought over yesterday." And he should have talked Lisette into spending these past two weeks here. Every time he was with her he felt better about things. But she would just look at him with those big green eyes and shake her head, as if she wondered where on earth he got his ideas.

"And Rosie should have stuck to arranging flowers instead of messing around in the kitchen. Her mind's not on cooking." Mac winked at him. "But things will be looking up in that direction, won't they?"

"Yeah. Looking up, all right." Cal could see the reflection of his king-size bed in the mirror and thought of his soon-to-be wife. He hadn't made love to her since Thanksgiving and he was damn sure looking forward to his wedding night, despite his nervous stomach right now. They were driving to Bozeman this afternoon, if the weather held. Two nights for a honeymoon wasn't going to be much, but Cal figured he'd take what he could get.

And he sure as hell would make the most of it.

"Your father would be real proud," Mac said, his voice raspy with emotion.

"Thanks." He squeezed the old man's shoulder and glanced over to see his mother standing in the doorway. She gave him the thumbs-up sign and then pointed to her watch.

Which meant it was time to get on with it.

"TIME TO GET READY. Aren't we supposed to be at the church in less than an hour?"

Lisette looked up from her work to see Maggie, dressed in a red suit, enter the kitchen. "I know. I'm trying to keep busy so I'm fussing at this."

"You're still in your bathrobe."

"I'm ready. All I have to do is put on my dress." She'd bought something new in Barstow last week, a forest green velvet dress with three-quarter length sleeves and a ballet neck. "And my ring. You look pretty."

"Thanks. I haven't been a matron of honor in years. Can I do anything?" She looked at the wedding cake and added, "Anything that doesn't have to do with food, that is."

Lisette laughed. "Maggie, I really could make a cook out of you, I promise."

"Nah," her friend said. "My mother said I was

hopeless and I still believe her." She stepped closer to the table. "It's beautiful."

"The baker should have a—" A fierce cramp hit her, stopping her words. Lisette took a deep breath when it was over and realized she'd dropped her knife on the floor.

"Lisette?" Maggie picked up the knife and set it in the sink. "Are you all right?"

"I'm not sure." It was the third time in the past hour that the pain had hit her and now Lisette had no choice but to believe that something was terribly wrong. "I'm having cramps," she said.

"You'd better sit down." Maggie pulled out a chair and helped Lisette into it.

She wrapped her arms around her abdomen as another pain hit. "I kept hoping the pain would stop. I thought it might be something I ate, but—" she gasped. "But I think it's getting worse."

"We need to get you to a doctor," Maggie said. "Where are the girls?"

"Upstairs. Mona's keeping them busy."

Maggie patted her shoulder. "I'm going to tell her what's going on and then I'm going to call Dr. Hawley. He's at the clinic on Saturdays."

"Thanks," Lisette said, suddenly feeling very cold. "Tell him I think I'm having a miscarriage." It even hurt to say the word.

"Don't move. I'll be right back."

"Maggie?" Lisette gripped the edge of the table as the next wave of pain ripped through her stomach and she felt the wetness between her legs. "I think it's too late."

CAL GOT THE NEWS from Maggie, who called the church office and managed to find someone to deliver a message. Lisette was ill and would he please go to the clinic. He left everyone and ran like hell down the street and up two blocks to where Doc Hawley stood smoking a cigarette on the front steps of the brick building.

"What's wrong?" Cal panted. "Where is she?"

"Hold on, son. Your, uh, fiancée has had a miscarriage." He took Cal's arm and forced him to sit down on the step. "When it happens this early in the pregnancy, it's often nature's way of stopping something that isn't right, you know that. You've raised enough cattle."

"Lisette isn't cattle."

"Nope. She's one real sad little lady right now, but you're going to go in there and tell her that it's okay and that you love her and the two of you will have lots of other babies."

He could do that, Cal thought.

"And then you're going to take her home and put her to bed and see that she gets some rest. She'll be weepy, but that's normal."

Normal, Cal repeated to himself. What was normal about losing a baby? He felt as if his heart had been sucked out of his body.

"She's to come in for a checkup next week. You want to wait a while before trying to get pregnant again," Doc said, tossing his cigarette into the box of sand by the door.

"Thanks, Doc." Cal saw his mother and Mac drive up in the Explorer SUV. They both looked scared to death, so he asked Doc to fill them in. "I need to go see Lisette."

"No problem. And remember, make her rest."

Rest. Tears. Normal. Nature's way. He tried to remember everything the doc said so he would know how to help Lisette. The nurse led him to a curtained area and allowed him to go inside. Maggie was there, but Lisette's eyes were closed. She looked as white as the hospital sheets tucked around her.

Maggie put a finger to her lips and, stopping to pat his arm, left him alone with the woman who should have married him by now. Was she relieved to be rid of him? Glad she wasn't going to have to raise another child? No. He leaned forward to see the traces of tears on her cheeks and Lisette opened her eyes.

"I'm sorry," she whispered.

"I know." He stroked her hair away from her face.

"It was over before I got here," she said, her eyes filling up with tears. "They couldn't do anything."

"It's okay. I'm going to take you home and see that you get some rest." Cal kissed her forehead.

"Not the ranch," she said, closing her eyes as if that would stop the tears from spilling out. "Anywhere but the ranch."

He wiped her tears with his thumbs, but Lisette moved away from his touch. "Maggie's going to take me home," Lisette said, opening her eyes but not looking at Cal. "You can go home now. You don't have to worry about me anymore."

The rejection stunned him almost as much as the miscarriage. "Whatever you want, sweetheart," Cal replied, remembering Hawley's advice. "Whatever you want is fine with me."

Much later, after he'd explained to their handful of guests that the wedding would have to be postponed, after he'd stopped at the bakery, after he'd driven his very disappointed family back to the ranch, and after he'd downed several shots of whiskey, Cal realized he didn't have to get married anymore. And that was when he locked himself in his office with a new bottle of Jack Daniel's whiskey.

LISETTE TOLD HERSELF it was for the best. She told herself she was better off without another child and another husband. She even told herself she never wanted to see Calder Brown again.

And for five long days she waited for him to come to her, so she could give back the ring. And coward that she knew she was, Lisette was glad when he didn't, so she wouldn't have to see the look of relief on his face when his commitment to her officially ended.

Loving him didn't mean she had to torture herself.

"BUT WHAT CAN WE DO?" Louisa asked, tossing her unplayed cards onto the table.

"I don't know, but we have to think of something. Mac said they haven't spoken to each other since the wedding." Ella didn't want to play gin rummy either, not this afternoon. She had no holiday spirit, despite Louisa's garish decorations on every spare mahogany surface. There was no meeting of the Hearts Club today, due to Missy's recent bout with the flu and Grace's last minute trip to Bozeman to shop.

"We have to think of some way to get them together, at least to talk, to see how much they belong together," Ella continued. "Something simple would be best."

"And if he doesn't love her after all," Louisa asked. "What do we do then?"

"He loves her," Ella declared. "If he didn't, he wouldn't be suffering so much."

Louisa didn't look convinced. Her eyes filled with tears and all three of her chins quivered. "Oh, Sister, I hope you're right."

Ella rolled her eyes. "Of course I am. Aren't I always?"

"WE NEED A CAKE," Mac told her, which surprised Lisette so much she almost dropped the phone. "For tonight. I know it's short notice, but is there any way you could do it?"

"Mac—" She began, knowing she had to refuse. "Don't do this."

"*He*'s not here, Lisette. One of the boys who works for us is getting married, so I'm throwing a little hoopla out here and—"

"Not the 'big cake,'" she interrupted. That wooden beast was newly decorated as a wedding cake and held a place of honor in the shop window. "It's retired."

"No, honey, not that. I'm looking for something to eat, something kinda fancy, though. Make it look like a ranch, with cowboys and horses and stuff."

"For what time?" She pulled out her order pad and grabbed a pencil. "And for how many people?"

"About twenty, I guess." The question seemed to confuse him. "Bring it on up around four-thirty, when you're done working. And bring the girls, too. The ponies miss 'em. And you're feeling better, I hear."

"I'm fine," she assured him.

"Well, we all sure wish it could've worked out different." Mac noisily cleared his throat. "You're taking good care of yourself?"

"Absolutely." She blinked back tears.

"I'll see you up here tonight?"

"I can't come to the ranch," she replied, though she wanted to ask how Cal was doing, where he'd been and was he as miserable as she was?

"Sure you can. My fool grandson isn't home," the old man said.

Later, of course, she realized Mac had lied.

"I'm sorry Mac deceived you," Cal said, sounding gruff and looking tired as he stood in the doorway of his kitchen. "I didn't know anything about this."

"No," she said. "I'm sure you didn't."

He looked as if he'd just gotten out of the shower after working a twelve-hour day. Cal eyed the cake she'd just finished assembling. "What the hell is that?"

"What your grandfather ordered for a party tonight."

"There's no party tonight."

"I guessed that." She eyed the two tier cake lined

with plastic fences and dotted with toy cowboys and horses in shades of yellow, green and blue. "He said he wanted something fancy that looked like a ranch."

"Tell me how you are," he said, not moving from the doorway.

"I'm doing fine," she fibbed, her attention still on the cake. She must have been crazy to buy blue horses.

"I've missed you."

"Really." She went over to the sink to wash the frosting off her fingers. "I hadn't noticed. I figured you must have been out celebrating."

"What?" She heard his footsteps, felt his hands on her shoulders as he spun her around to face him. "Celebrate what, exactly?"

"Your freedom." She tried to sound casual. "Look, Cal, we both know we're better off this way, without having to get married because of a broken—"

"Don't say another word." His hands gripped her shoulders so she couldn't move away. "Just listen for a minute. I wanted to come to see you—I *did* come to see you—but I didn't know what to say to make things better. And I was afraid I'd say the wrong thing and make you cry, make you feel even worse. And then I started thinking that maybe you were happy to get rid of me and that about drove me crazy."

"Me, too," she managed to say. "You should have been jumping for joy, you know."

"No. Never that."

"I guess we both feel like we missed out on something," she whispered, still wishing for something she wasn't going to hear. Lisette ducked out of his grasp and moved sideways. "I'm glad we talked."

He frowned. "That's it?"

Lisette stopped and looked up at him. "I married a man who secretly had two other wives, two fiancées and three more children. When we all discovered each other and the story broke, the tabloids called us 'The Hart-less Wives.' It was supposed to be clever."

"I hope the s.o.b. is in jail."

"He is," she said. "For a very long time, because he also embezzled money and was convicted of tax evasion. But you can see why I didn't leap at the idea of marrying you, someone with a reputation with the ladies."

"But you were. Marrying me, that is."

"Because I fell in love with you, you idiot. That's the only reason. Not the baby and not your enormous ranch and not because we're good in bed together—"

"Great," he said, moving closer to her. "*Great* in

bed together, which gives me an idea. Are the girls still outside riding their ponies with Mac?"

"Don't tease, Cal." She put her hands on her hips. "I'm a bit edgy these days."

"Kitchen sex is fun," he insisted, stepping forward so he backed her against the counter. "I remember making love to a Frenchwoman underneath that very table over there."

"Cal—"

"I think that's when I fell in love with her," he whispered. "First time in my life, too. I was so new at falling in love that I acted like a real idiot."

"Yes," she said, lifting her mouth for the kiss that was sure to come. "You certainly had your moments."

"But I've changed," he said, tickling her lips with his own. "I'm going to be the best damn husband and father in Bliss."

"Is that a proposal?" His body was hot against hers, making thinking difficult.

"Sweetheart, come to my bedroom and find out."

Lisette did.

CALL THE ONES YOU LOVE OVER THE HOLIDAYS!

Save $25 off future book purchases when you buy any four Harlequin® or Silhouette® books in October, November and December 2001,

PLUS

receive a phone card good for 15 minutes of long-distance calls to anyone you want in North America!

WHAT AN INCREDIBLE DEAL!

Just fill out this form and attach 4 proofs of purchase (cash register receipts) from October, November and December 2001 books, and Harlequin Books will send you a coupon booklet worth a total savings of $25 off future purchases of Harlequin® and Silhouette® books, AND a 15-minute phone card to call the ones you love, anywhere in North America.

Please send this form, along with your cash register receipts
as proofs of purchase, to:
In the USA: Harlequin Books, P.O. Box 9057, Buffalo, NY 14269-9057
In Canada: Harlequin Books, P.O. Box 622, Fort Erie, Ontario L2A 5X3
Cash register receipts must be dated no later than December 31, 2001.
Limit of 1 coupon booklet and phone card per household.
Please allow 4-6 weeks for delivery.

**I accept your offer! Please send me my
coupon booklet and a 15-minute phone card:**

Name: _____

Address: _____ City: _____

State/Prov.: _____ Zip/Postal Code: _____

Account Number (if available): _____

---

097 KJB DAGL
PHQ4012